MALKI PRESS

The Philistines Be Upon Thee

Stephen Toman

Published by Malki Press, Edinburgh.

Copyright © Stephen Toman, 2019

The right of Stephen Toman to be identified as author of this Work has been asserted by him in accordance with sections 77 and 78 of the Copyright, Designs and Patents Act 1988.
All rights reserved. No part of this book may be reproduced without prior permission from the author or publisher.

This book is a work of fiction and therefore any resemblance to real persons or situations is coincidental.

ISBN: 9781686780134

The Philistines Be Upon Thee

Stephen Toman

For Doff

"Men thus ingenious and inquisitive were content to live in total ignorance of the trades by which human wants are supplied, and to supply them by the grossest means . . . the culture of their lands was unskilful, and their domestick life unformed; their tables were coarse as the feasts of Eskimeaux, and their houses filthy as the cottages of Hottentots."

—SAMUEL JOHNSON

"And I see too much
And I broke my face
And my head grows too much.

God spits
On my soul
There's something dead inside my hole"

—THE JESUS AND MARY CHAIN
"In My Hole," *Psychocandy*

In which the 19th Countess of Sutherland, Lady Elizabeth Gordon, surveys her inheritance and ponders what to do with the pesky tenants living on her land and compares the sweetness of her husband's urine to that of another man.

THE 19ᵀᴴ COUNTESS OF SUTHERLAND TWIRLED HER umbrella absent-mindedly, creating an impression, for anyone who was to observe her at that moment, of levity or gaiety at odds with, firstly, the weather, for it was, in the local vernacular, pishin it doon, and, secondly, the graveness of the proceedings, whilst she perambulated the fringe of her inheritance. Her husband was out shooting grouse with the chief's hand, the strong, quiet man she had been introduced to the night before (she felt her face turning pink at the thought, though with the lashing it was receiving from the summer rain and wind, no-one would notice). She touched the back of a gloved hand to her cheek and felt some relief at its coolness.

McSwine, the chief, was resetting the soaked and frankly ridiculous bonnet on his head for the umpteenth time, accompanied, as always, by two guards carrying his ceremonial shield. He was handsome once, if the portraits hanging in his mansion could be trusted (though it was not unheard of for artists to flatter those who had commissioned them). He had been drinking, clearly. She had been offered a skalk of whisky with her breakfast but declined, sick at the thought, having imbibed one too many the previous night. One too many being a single heavily-peated number from one of the islands, which sent her to bed with a migraine after a single sip. Gone were the days of round the clock drinking where she was from. Her father's generation had been the last. When business decisions, contracts, and other financial agreements were made in an ale house, an environment that lent itself too easily to exaggeration and to aggression, all too often no-one could quite remember what it was they had agreed to or the reasons why an unusual or specific clause had been included in a deal and, if it had been written down, were unable to read it. No, with the introduction of coffee and, subsequently, the coffee house, the Gordons now made their arrangements sober and with their wits not only about them but improved, stimulated by the effects of caffeine and sugar, her husband's pissing disease an unfortunate, yet preferred, side-effect compared with the alcoholic afflictions of her now (mercifully) deceased father, whose affinity for the bottle was the cause of his ill-health and yet, ironically, also the source of his longevity. The countess imagined him preserved in a giant, invisible pickling jar. She waved a hand in the direction of the aqueduct.

They stood on the hillside looking down into the valley where Badwater sat on the banks of a loch, also called Badwater. The loch disappeared into cloud where it reached the sea, the waves crashing against the ragged clifftop, all that separated the two bodies of water, taking with it farming equipment, bits of houses, even animals from the village of Badbae perched atop it.

"The aqueduct is coming along nicely, I see," said the countess.

"It is indeed," replied her commissioner, standing proudly, legs askance, hands clasped behind his back, tweed jacket too tight. (Has he put on weight? she wondered.)

"You look like a sheepdog walker," she said.

"You mean a shepherd, ma'am."

"Yes, of course," she tittered, "silly me," thinking about how his piss was not as pleasant-tasting as her husband's but that his cock certainly remained harder for longer.

It was left to Sellar to arrange the evictions, he being more familiar with the rights of tenants and whatnot than the commissioner, who had been tasked by the Lady's husband to make arrangements with the chief regarding the land that was his wife's inheritance but instead spent the majority of his time hunting and fishing and making plans for his own spot of land that had been given to him in gratitude by his mistress. Immediately he had purchased and filled the estate with sheep, which seemed, to him, better suited to living in the primitive crofts than the human occupants. He assumed the crofters would become disgruntled to find themselves sharing their homes with the animals and leave, but they barely noticed, finding the sheep irksome at most. Sellar took care of it, however. He only had to burn down one of the crofts before the other tenants took what they could carry and moved to Badbae.

"The canal is considerably behind schedule," said Sellar, dressed as usual in his suit and overcoat. "I have been corresponding with the architect regarding compensation for interference with our—I mean, your—business operations here."

The chief looked like someone had kicked him up the arse, swollen nose more bulbous and veiny than usual.

"You've been what?"

"Thank you, Sellar," said Elizabeth. "Some form of compensation would be a useful contribution to the setting up of factories here. Labourers and materials and whatnot."

"Factories?" spat McSwine.

Sellar looked at him with disgust.

"I assume from your demeanor, Randall, that you are not happy with the Lady Gordon's notion of developing Badwater into a centre of industry?"

"What are you haverin about, lad? Sheep and kelp?"

"We plan, Mister McSwine," said Elizabeth, softly-spoken but firm, "for a herring fishery, salt pans, possibly coal—or shale—and perhaps a tile or brick works. We have the necessary associations back home and we will all profit considerably from these ventures. Yourself included. But," she wrinkled her nose, "these will have to go." She flicked a gloved hand in the direction of the crofts dotting the hillside as though to shoo them away. "Why people would choose to live in such squalor baffles me. Look at that one!" She pointed to a small dwelling made entirely of loosely assembled flat rocks, with a ceiling of dirt and turf that had partially fallen in from its own increasing weight. "It doesn't even have any windows."

"People who are not used to such comforts do not

miss them." The commissioner looked at the chief as he said this. The chief responded by grunting and taking from his coat pocket a flask that he drank from without pleasure.

"They will have to go."

Replacing the cork into the neck of the flask, the chief just shook his head.

"Sellar?"

"My Lady?"

"Can you take care of them?"

"There is a settlement on the coast. Many tenants have moved there already. In fact, many of them work for you, burning kelp."

"They are working? Oh, I am pleased to hear that!"

"Accommodation in exchange for labour, my Lady. A similar arrangement as they had with the chief."

"They have no use for money here, Elizabeth," said the commissioner. "Why, where would they spend it?"

He giggled, Elizabeth tittered. The chief uncorked his flask and drank again, grimacing.

"It will be useful to have such a . . ." she hunted for the right word ". . . willing workforce when we expand our interests in the region." She smiled.

"If they don't fuck off to America first."

"Excuse me?"

"What did you say?" shouted the commissioner with a hand to his belt where he kept a holster for a pistol he had not yet hit anything with. "I kindly ask you to show some courtesy in front of a lady. Scottish or not, you are being disrespectful."

Elizabeth frowned and flicked her hand again as

though the word "fuck" hung in the air before her and she was merely brushing it aside. Where others might have grown fearful of it and cowered, awaiting saviour by a noble gentleman from this filthy word, she was unfazed.

"What do you mean? Are your people moving to America?"

Sellar, interrupting: "Some of the clansmen have previously bought passage to America. But the journey is dangerous. It is long and extremely arduous and conditions are poor. It is cramped, not to mention prohibitively expensive. I have it on good authority that some ships are known to take money from families only to throw them overboard when they reach the ocean. Or worse, sell them into slavery. To be perfectly honest," he continued, "none of the crofters seem particularly interested in leaving. They might mention it in anger every now and then but they soon talk themselves out of it. There are too many uncertainties. By and large, they seem to be content with their lot these days. There may come a time where their only course of action is violence but if and when that time comes *our* only course of action will be the same. And we will win."

A VILE COUNTRY,
TO BE SURE

—When I left that day I didn't know that it would be the last time I'd see my folks or that I was about to walk more than a hundred miles just to watch my brother die. I suppose, at the back of my mind, I suspected that my father might not hang in there till I got back, but not my mother. If I'd known, I would have given her a proper cuddle but I didn't want to seem weak.

That's not true.

If I had known it was the last time I'd see them then I wouldn't have gone. Probably. But then I'd be dead as well.

I met Sugar on the canal. You couldn't miss him. Big lad, this huge red beard. Neither was unusual. His skin, however, was this blue-grey-green, his whole body tattooed. And the ink from them had bled so that you couldn't see the true colour of his skin but it wasn't white like mine. Like mine used to be.

He showed up one day and asked for work. The

gaffer gave him a shovel and told him to dig a hole, such-and-such by such-and-such, and timed him doing so. He didn't seem bothered at all by the work but when the whistle blew for lunch and at the end of the day, he'd drop his spade or his pick, just leave it where he dropped it, and go join the queue for lunch or to get his *per diem* for dinner, which he spent on ale or whisky, depending on how hungry he was. If he was hungry he had ale, otherwise it was whisky. It was usually whisky he had. Only thing I ever saw him eat was the porridge the Company served for breakfast and the oatcakes and hard cheese they handed out at lunch.

Sugar ended up in the gaol the same night me and my brother did. My father had gone down to the hotel after his boat got in and he heard we'd been arrested. There he confronted the three excisemen who'd found us. Versions of events differ—some say that my father attacked one of them with a knife, that he broke their arm and slashed their face, stuck the knife right into their cheek and tore it so his face flapped open like a burst tent and you could see his back teeth; others that the men's guards done him in before he even had the opportunity to speak—but, either way, my father ended up half-dead outside in the street beside our horse, which they gutted.

How Sugar ended up there that night was just coincidence. He was at the hotel and had seen what happened to my father but the innkeeper told him to stay out of it. But then, afterwards, when the two excisemen were having a celebratory drink for apprehending my brother and me and nearly killing my father—the third one was taken away to get fixed up—

Sugar had tried to pay for his drinks with the dinner token the Company gave us when they banned us from drinking, but when the innkeeper told him he couldn't pay with that, Sugar had gotten angry, and the excisemen became interested, and so did their guards, so Sugar took a bottle of whisky from behind the bar and, holding it like a dinner bell, drove the end of it into one of the guard's faces. The guard took his beating silently, unable even to groan in pain from the blood that spilled into his open mouth from his splintering nose, till the bottle broke. Then Sugar dropped him and left. The sucking of dark blood through the guard's ruptured facade was the only indication that he was still alive.

He got let off in the end. The Company intervened, said the canal was behind schedule and that they needed all the workers they could get. So me and Sugar ended up working inside one of the boxes on the loch, constructing the legs of the bridge the canal was to go over. The canal was supposed to merge with the loch but—the story went—they'd forgotten to take into account the height difference, some argument over contour lines, so when they had dug it as far as the hills behind Badwater they saw that the loch was quite a distance below.

My brother, he got taken away to be sentenced.

The box was just what it sounds like. Made of wood, open at the top and higher than any building I'd ever seen, it floated on a raft and we lived and worked inside it. The inside of it had been tarred to make it waterproof and one of our jobs was to make sure it stayed that way. You had to climb up a ladder on the outside to get to the opening at the top and then you had to climb down onto the scaffolding inside of it. Inside the box we were to build the leg of the bridge the canal was to go over. Stone bricks were brought to us by boat and lowered down inside the box by a pulley and we would line them up on the floor of the raft, tight against the walls, construct the leg of the bridge from the inside. With every stone the raft and the box would sink a little. By the time the weight of the stone was enough to pull the whole thing under we'd built the leg of the bridge high enough so that it stuck out of the water—just a couple of feet above, seemingly forever, until enough of the leg had been built that it reached all the way to the bottom of the loch. Then we could start building up the way.

Nobody spoke much inside the box. There was about eight of us in there at first but it dropped to six, then just to four of us, I think, by the time the weight of the stone had sunk us to the bottom of the loch. Folk got sick—headaches, dizziness, pains in their chest—and had to get pulled out.

First time I spoke to Sugar properly was one night after work. I was putting off climbing back inside the box. The thought alone was making me light-headed. My joints hurt and it wasn't just from building. I was used to that. Felt like my bones themselves were going to burst. Sugar was sitting at the top of the leg, facing Badbae, out towards the open sea, his legs dangling over the edge like he was thinking about jumping. The sun was dipping behind the hills. You could see the other legs of the bridge, the other boxes, these black monoliths jutting out of the glassy water. Other workers were doing the same as us, watching the sun set, trying to talk themselves into climbing back down into the dark to get some rest. Three legs had been completed, two of which were linked by the dry canal bed running over them, another couple protruding from the water at different heights, but the one in the middle—though it was started the same time as the others—rose only a few feet and had been that way for some time. Folk had rowed out and looked inside and, while they reported that the stone walls had been constructed, saw only darkness, no light or sign of scaffolding and received no reply to their calls. Messages had been lowered on string that, when raised, were gone but no response ever came back (though this in itself was not unusual given that not many of us could read or write). The raft with building materials was still tied to the leg and its stock lessened daily, though, by whom, no one ever saw. Bread and cheese and some ale, too, were lowered in buckets every week (when some could be spared) and were gone when the buckets were raised, though air had long since stopped being pumped inside. Some said the folk inside had still not reached the bottom of the loch, that the raft, the box and the stone leg were still slowly sinking, pulling them under so they had no choice but to keep building to avoid the whole construction being pulled beneath the surface and the water pouring in over the top—*no even stopping to sleep or eat or huv a shite*—always building. Others said they'd reached the bottom yonks ago but, instead of building upwards, started digging, tunneling through clay and stone, though nobody could ever suggest a reason for why they'd do this.

I remembered I had a flask in my pocket and took it out. Sugar must have heard the pop of the cork and turned around.

—Want some? I offered him the flask.

—What is it? he said, taking it from me.

—Whisky.

He sniffed the opening.

—Smells like piss, he said.

The flask was a pig's bladder. I hadn't done a good job of curing it.

He took a swig, thought about it for a bit before swallowing.

—It's good, he said. Salty, smoky, sweet. Nicely offset by a bouquet of piss.

—Thanks. Made it myself.

Well, my brother did. But I helped.

He tossed the flask back to me and I nearly dropped it. The bottom of the box was full of water. Not that deep but I never would have found the flask again in the dark. I replaced the cork and went to put the flask back in my pocket.

—You're not having any, Sugar said.

I shrugged.

—Give it back then.

His hand shook when he held it out. I tossed it to him. He nodded thanks, popped the cork.

When he finished, he weighed the flask in one hand. Then he threw it into the water.

—Is there more?

—Not now, no.

I told him about my brother. He gave no indication that he was listening.

That night it rained and the box filled with water and we lost all our tools. I sat shivering in soaking clothes on my shelf. I slept near the bottom. Less dizzy down there and the headaches weren't as bad. Seemed to sleep better too. Maybe because I was less worried about falling.

Sugar was trying to get my attention. I couldn't hear him over the noise of the rain rattling on the stone, into the water. He was shouting.

I looked around for the ladder. Couldn't keep my eyes open. The water streamed down my face.

—Climb, I heard him shout.

He pointed. The water was rising. I took hold of the ladder but I was shivering so much I struggled to hold it. I could barely hear Sugar over my chattering teeth. I put my foot on the ladder and pulled myself up. Fingers were too cold, I couldn't hold on. My hand slipped, then my foot. I looped my arm round a rung and fumbled with my other hand, tried to get a foot on but couldn't. I wrapped my legs round the ladder and clung on. The water had reached my feet. Rain cascaded over me. I felt the cold creep up my body.

Sugar's arm was around me before I heard his voice in my ear. Seemed like I was floating when he lifted me above the water line and laid me down on the scaffolding.

—We should be okay here, he said.

We were still far from the top.

—You need to take these off, he said.

I was too cold to resist.

—You need to be dry.

When he lifted my shirt over my head he turned away. He handed me a blanket without looking back. The blanket was damp but drier than I was. I couldn't stop shaking, thought my teeth were going to break from clacking against one another.

His clothes were wet too. He sat back on his heels and looked at me swaddled in the blanket. Then he took off his clothes and slid under the blanket and put his arms around me.

By morning the rain had stopped. I looked down at the water that filled the box. There was a body floating in it.

—Our tools are down there, I said.

Sugar was dressed. His clothes were still wet.

—No work today, he said. Not unless you can swim.

I shook my head.

—Can you? I asked.

He didn't say that he could.

We climbed out and waited for a boat to come and get us, let our clothes dry in the sun.

—Thanks, I said.

Sugar didn't look at me, just raised and lowered one shoulder.

—What's your name? I asked.

—People call me Sugar, he said after a while.

I held out my hand to shake his. Only then did he look at me for the first time since he pulled me out of the water.

I told him my name was Heifer.

He took my hand.

—Actually, it's Aoife but when I was born my brother couldn't get it right, kept calling me Heifer instead. Like the cow.

—Eva, he said.

—Aoife, I repeated.

—Evil, he said. Then he shook my hand and looked

me in the eye. It only dawned on me then that he had taken me for a boy.

—Aye, that'll do, I said. Call me Evil.

He smiled.

Maybe he didn't. I can't see him smiling, now I think about it. I can't picture myself doing it either, though I know I must have.

—Heifer, he said and let go of my hand.

So we went back to working on the hill, churning up dirt and stone. I slept there with the rest of the workers, too tired at the end of the day to make it worth the trek back to Badbae. Ma would just worry when she saw me falling asleep at the dinner table and my father, well, he didn't know if I was there or not.

It wasn't long before that work stopped too. The foreman had an accident. He was packing a rock full of gunpowder when it must have sparked and exploded and the tamping iron he'd been using to pack the gunpowder went straight through his skull. I saw it happen. He had been crouching to light the fuse when the tamping iron shot out the top of his head, knocking his hat off. He stood up, took a few steps backwards and stumbled, fell twitching with his tongue slapping the roof of his mouth, this sucking sound, saliva bubbles, lips all twisted.

After a minute or two of us wondering what we should do with his dead body, he sat up and looked about for his bowler. A little blood trickled from the entrance in his check, this pink mess and bone dust on the ground behind him. He held out his hand and someone rushed forward to take it and helped him to his feet whilst another fetched his hat and handed it to him. The foreman took it, nodded thanks and threw up, and, when he did, you could see the pulsations of his brain as it squeezed out the hole.

The accountant got a couple of workers to carry the foreman home and sent another to get the minister. Everyone else he told to get back to work, to get those boulders cleared.

This is, so the story goes, what happened next:

Using a knife bathed in week-old whisky the minister scraped a protrusion of brain from the cleaned skull of the foreman like a bartender smoothing the head of an overfilled glass of ale. The foreman sat on the edge of his bed and barely winced while the minister removed dried blood and bone fragments from the opening. When the minister had finished and had applied a cold compress and instructed the foreman to remain upright, the foreman thanked him and asked him to pass on his apologies to the Company, expressing his displeasure at the necessity of having to take a couple days off work to convalesce.

After a restless night, the minister returned early the next morning and found himself having to wake the foreman's young wife, who took comfort in her brave husband's progress and had slept soundly, but where the foreman had previously been lucid—if oddly ambivalent about the severity of his injury—he was now clinically and certifiably (had the minister actually been a doctor) insane, chattering endlessly and inanely and not making any sense whatsoever, although the minister did take solace in that the words spoken by the foreman were genuine words, even if they were not being used in any logical order or context.

The tissue around the foreman's eye was swollen and the eye itself now protruded considerably so that the widest part of its circumference lay outside the socket itself, resting on it like an egg in an eggcup or a golf ball on a tee. And his breath was atrocious. Fetid, rotten, like a sausage stored in an uncleaned stomach and forgotten about in a wet leather satchel for several days, weeks.

He took off the dressing and gagged at the smell as he scoured more brain matter from the foreman's scalp, cleaned it again and applied a fresh dressing, wondering—and feeling guilty for doing so—how much longer he would be required to keep up this ordeal before the man succumbed to his fate.

Each day the minister knocked on the door of the foreman's house, waking the young wife who greeted him sleepily but cheerfully and made—in spite of the circumstances (and the smell)—some delightful coffee, wondering if this would be the day when he would hold the man's hand and offer reassurances of the afterlife as he passed from this one, or—better yet— arrived to the young wife opening the door clutching a handkerchief, red-eyed and sobbing, the foreman having slipped away in his sleep, but instead spent the morning wiping puss and brain from the man's scalp while he babbled frivolously, using words of work and politics as well as the odd expletive for which he would add *Sorry, Father,* sometimes before he said it, all the while becoming more adept at putting together the pieces of the foreman's verbal brain-jigsaw, when, one morning, the door was opened, not by the young wife, but by the foreman himself, whose eye, by this point, was so engorged with infection that, when he sneezed, which he soon did, left the confines of its socket entirely. The foreman was dressed for work and was wearing his hat but had yet to put on his coat. Or his trousers.

—Y-you're . . . feeling better?

—Oh yes, the foreman smiled, much better thank you.

—Are you . . . planning on returning to work?

—Why of course.

—You might want to take a few more days rest. Let that eye heal.

—This one? The foreman prodded it with an index finger. Ach, every time I squeeze it back in it just pops out again. I think I'll just leave it where it is for now.

The eye watched him, sitting there upon the foreman's cheekbone.

He invited him in for coffee and the minister sat at the small wooden table while the foreman smashed dried beans in muslin with a rolling pin and shook them into a pot of hot water. Without spilling a drop he poured the coffee straight from the pot into two mugs, leaving the spent grounds behind. The minister blew on his and took a tentative sip, initially only out of politeness but found it to be pleasant, nearly as good as that which the foreman's wife usually served. Speaking of the foreman's wife, where was she?

—Your wife's out early, he said.

—She's still in bed.

—Ah. She'll need the rest I suppose.

—She's dead father. I killed her.

Too polite to spit the coffee from his mouth in surprise, the minister swallowed it in a single gulp and his eyes streamed while it burned its way through his oesophagus.

The foreman had wanted to return to work but his wife, with good reason, and in spite of her naive indifference to the severity of his injury, did not think he was ready, that he should at least wait for his eye to recede back into its socket and for at least some of his brain to stop leaking from his head. He would wear a hat, he told her, but she insisted. He didn't argue or retort, just stood dumbly in the kitchen with his tongue lolling in his mouth, brain protruding from his skull like a hemorrhoid, and did what he usually did when an immovable object got in the way of his work. That night, while she was sleeping, reassured by her husband's silent agreement to rest a little longer, the foreman packed his wife full of gunpowder and lit the fuse. He had taken precise measurements and used only the amount he needed to demolish the young woman so that when the minister opened the bedroom door, which had remained securely on its hinges, he found everything to be in its usual place—ornaments on the windowsill, candles on the dresser, the Holy Bible . . . only the cracked glass of the window and the charred outline of a body on the bed sheet and the foreman's wife torn into a million pieces and scattered around the room like rose petals, obliterated, was not typical.

The minister closed the bedroom door and stifled a retch with his fist. The foreman beamed.

When they apprehended him he didn't resist, let them lead him into his cell in the gaol.

—Oh my goodness, Sellar had squealed. Can I keep him?

The gaoler just looked at him, then at the chief, and back to the foreman. The chief breathed deeply, pulling at his whiskers, and sighed.

—What do we do with him?

The foreman shuffled inside his cage, stopping now and then to smile inquisitively at his visitors.

—If it was up to me, started the chief.
—It is up to you, replied the minister.
—There are laws governing—
—What's your point?
—As I was saying—if it was up to me—
—It is up to you.
—It is not up to me. We are governed by—
—You were saying?
—He's obviously ill. Not right in the head, I mean. If he was an animal—

The foreman, who was still wearing his bowler hat, removed it and scratched his wound with a finger, digging in until his finger had disappeared to the second knuckle.

—Dear God.
—What you're saying is we should put him out of his misery? Is that right?
—Yes. Well, no. I mean, if he was an animal—

The foreman sucked goop from his finger.

—with an injury like that—
—He is an animal.
—He is a human being, Mister Sellar! The minister's mouth hung agape. Like you or I.
—Yes, he agreed. Us too.
—Are you referring to me as an animal, Sellar? asked the chief. What animal would that be then?

Sellar ignored him.

—Human beings are not animals.
—Could an animal do what I do? the chief asked.
—Couldn't do any worse if you ask me, said the minister.
—Well what are we then? Vegetables? Bricks?
—Well . . .
—We eat, we shit, we shag—some us do—and we

sleep. We're animals. Some of us kill, too.

—And some of us—nodding towards the cage—hold our nose and squeeze brain through a hole in the top of our skull and pick off bits of it to chew on like tobacco, said the gaoler.

—There would need to be a trial, said Sellar.

—Where?

—A crime of this magnitude would go to the High Court. Though he will likely be hanged, unless a plea can be made for insanity. I suppose I could be his lawyer.

—You? The chief and his brother asked together.

—Yes. My very own idiot.

In the end they let him go. Returned his hat and tamping rod. You could hear him exploding bits of the hill, day and night. Dirt and stone would rain down into town or a farmer would find a sheep or two exploded and someone would have to go find him and tell him to get the fuck away from where there's people and animals. Sometimes things would explode on their own but more than likely the foreman was just experimenting with lengths of wire. One time, an explosion occurred that took out some of the reservoir wall and sent water down the half-dug canal bed and over the unfinished aqueduct. But while this was happening the gaffer was nursing a glass of milk at the hotel bar.

People asked:

—Was that you?

—How on earth did you do that?

But the gaffer just grinned and tipped his hat and kept the spool of wire hidden up his sleeve.

When I got back to our hut on Badbae the minister was there. He had come every day since the beating, on his way to and from visiting the foreman. The minister was wiping my father's brow with a wet cloth. When the soldiers had grown tired and stopped just short of killing him, God had picked up from where they left off. His jaw swung from its hinges and the bones beneath the skin of his head was lumpy and the rest of his body worse. And he was stricken with fever. By the time the minister got to him there was not a lot he could do but pray none of the wounds became infected. Father couldn't eat, could barely breathe or talk. He supped water from a wet piece of cloth draped across his mouth.

My grandfather was sitting at the wee table, smoking and shaking his head. All he ever did. He had gone to speak to the chief but ended up speaking to Sellar. Sellar was the one that moved us out to Badbae, balanced on the narrow ledge of rock between the sea and the loch, where we had nowhere even to lash our boat that didn't end with it being reduced to splinters by morning, where mothers had to decide whether to risk their bairns being blown by the fierce wind into the sea on one side or the loch on the other or keep them inside huts that collapsed daily, hemmed between drystone walls to keep us separate from the sheep, winds that battered the cliffs till they broke apart and fell away in chunks to the sea, fishing boats smashed against the rocks or lost during the night. It was not unheard of for the remains of a boat that left Badbae full of men to be returned empty. Soon after we moved somebody's horse was carried over the cliff and its carcass lay mangled on the loch-side rocks. All that was left of it was a rib cage submerged in a shallow pool and some swirling matted hair. Ploughs turned over rock after rock, seeds scattered by the wind or their leaves thrashed into submission. We caught some shellfish from the rocks and got some butter and cheese, a little meat, on occasion, should an animal die of natural causes, such as plummeting onto the rocks below, which was happening so often some of the crofters took to tethering their animals to posts buried in the ground. Children as well could be seen in high winds billowing like kites between similarly buoyant livestock. Nothing would grow in the salted earth. Soon we ran out of grain, out of butter, and had nothing to trade. We dried the meat, not knowing when we would next have some, but it gave whoever ate it a case of the shites so bad it raised the question of whether it was worth eating at all. But we did, assuring each other that the gutrot we washed it down with would kill any sickness, if we weren't caught in possession of it first, in which case you wouldn't have to worry about shiteing yourself to death.

The chief had refused to see my grandfather but Sellar said he would write a letter, acting as our brother's lawyer.

—Being the chief's lawyer effectively makes him ours as well, said my grandfather. Told me that if we could get enough money together to pay the tax and the fine then we might be able to get him off.

My father always said that Sellar was a cunt.

Alexander! my mother would say, using his full name.

My father would say sorry, then, after a wee pause would go, He is a cunt but. He wasn't well enough to say it then so my grandfather said it instead.

—The man's a cunt.

—Alexander!

Alexander was also my grandfather's name. And my brother's. It could get confusing. Might as well just call us by our last names like they did in town. My father was Lawdun or Big Lawdun, my grandfather was Big Lawdun or Auld Lawdun, and my brother was Wee Lawdun, but he was bigger than the other two so folk took to calling him either just Lawdun or Big Man. I was Lawdun's Wee Sister.

My mother waited for the minister's reaction but he just shrugged and said, Aye, if ever a man was a cunt, it's him. My brother as well.

His brother was the chief.

—They're all cunts, said my grandfather.

My mother shook her head. Behind the curtain I knew my father was smiling.

The minister took his hat from the table and held it against his chest while he looked at my mother. Her eyes were red. He put a hand on her shoulder, smiled and put on his hat. He nodded at me and left.

The letter was brought by the chief's one-eye, naked but for a bit of rope tied round his waist. He said that my brother was being held in a gaol in the city and that if we could get enough money together quickly, they might be able to settle the fine before he faced trial. None of us could read the letter. We had to take the word of the messenger.

My grandfather spat, black globule of tobacco and saliva stretching from the hinge of the wooden gate he swung on.

—Look at them. Hairy, black-faced bastards. That land there used to be ours.

—They're only sheep, Granda.

—Look at them, the cords on his neck were straining, look at their content wee faces. I bet they sleep with both eyes closed too.

He leaned over the fence.

—Don't get too comfortable! They'll kick you off it, same as they did us. Took the clothes from our backs and fucked us up the arse so hard their cocks flopped out our mouths like coo's tongues—

—Granda!

The tobacco-laden globule of black spit finally stretched too far and broke off the hinge, landing on my foot.

—Sake, I said, wiping it on the grass.

—Where are your shoes?

—I don't have any.

—Whit?

—They fell to bits. When I was workin in the box. Could never get them dry so they just fell apart. Ma's no had a chance to make new ones.

He looked away.

—You've a long walk, lass, and you'll be needin them. It's about time you started makin your own anyway. I'll show you how.

—Aye.

—You'll need somebody to go with you.

I had somebody in mind. Didn't know if they would do it though.

—Are you not coming?

—Those days are behind me, lass.

We turned away from the sheep, looked out at the stretch of rock we called home.

—You know your ma's pregnant, he said.

I'd noticed but never acknowledged a sibling till it could breathe on its own and even then I'd helped bury more than one. Nothing grows on Badbae.

Sugar was sitting in his tent on the hill, looking out to sea, when I asked him.

—Do you ever think they'll finish this? he said.

I assumed he was referring to the aqueduct.

—Not if all the navvy are as lazy as you.

He didn't say anything else but I replied as though he had.

—My father's dying and my mother is pregnant and my brother's in gaol. How's yourself?

—Your father is dying? he asked eventually.

—He's not got long left. I'm heading south with a cart full of illegal whisky I need to sell to pay my brother's fine and get him out of gaol. I need your help.

—Me specifically?

—I'm asking you.

—And if I say no?

—Then I don't know who else to ask.

—Why should I?

I gave him a flask of whisky.

—For this?

I shook my head.

—That's just 'cause I know you like it. And I had some spare.

He pulled out the cork, sniffed the opening and drank.

—I wouldn't do it. I mean if I were you. I don't think.

—Still good, he said, referring to the whisky.

—Look, I said, there's no reason why you should help me. I'll probably still go myself even if you don't come. But it'll be easier if you do. And whatever's left after I pay the fine is yours to keep. You won't even have to see us back here.

Sugar took another drink.

—What else are you going to do?

—What's he in jail for?

I put my hand out for the flask and when he gave me it I drank till it was empty.

—Making whisky.

The plan was simple: take all the whisky we could to the city and sell it, use the profits to get my brother out of jail and bring him home.

The old man knew the route, he and my father had done it many times before. Used to do it openly, before it was illegal. They would travel as far as they needed to, trade the whisky they made for animals, feed, cloth, whathaveyou. Only when the businesses and the landowners and the excisemen started coming did my father and my grandfather have to start doing it on the fly, trading locally and selling it further away.

I'd never made the journey before. My brother had. And was doing it again in chains.

Seeing as the horse was dead I had to take the cow to pull the cart. The cart was piled high with jars and barrels of whisky—everything we had. In amongst that sat the metal lady, whisky sloshing in her belly, in her arms and legs. From a distance, draped in a shawl, it looked like she was pregnant. Just a pregnant lady riding in a cart pulled by a cow, an uncommon but not unheard of sight around these parts. Sugar and me walked alongside her. We wore soldiers' uniforms. Stole them from a couple lads on leave. Poisoned them.

—The key is to throw the heather in after it boils, said my grandfather. Then it infuses the beer with mystical properties that would otherwise be boiled off. It's a very pleasant experience, I'm told.

He was tearing at a branch of heather, separating the flowers and tossing them into a barrel. I gathered up an entire bush and dumped it into the frothing ale.

—Is this really going to work? asked Sugar.

My grandfather shrugged without moving his shoulders.

—Worst case scenario, they get the shites so bad they'll not be able to stand up.

At the end of the week we rolled the barrel to the inn where the two soldiers were staying.

Before leaving that morning they were invited by the innkeeper to toast a safe journey back to the fort.

—On the house, he told them, serving each of them a pint of the mystical ale.

The soldiers thanked him and washed down their breakfast of oatcakes and soft cheese.

The innkeeper offered them a second pint, which they accepted graciously, even asking and paying for more to fill their flasks with before leaving.

The soldiers took the winding path up past the aqueduct and followed the route of the canal, keeping to the flattened grass and earth, wading through the seas and undulating hillocks of moss, before turning onto the soldiers' road,

On more than one occasion each saw the other look behind him but when asked about what it was they saw they would say nothing. And yet both of them felt it, that sense of being watched, followed, by a green figure close behind that arose from the ground in long, silent strides and sunk back into the soil between steps.

They stopped to lie down with their heads resting against their packs, sipping from the strange brew the innkeeper had given them, and the figure emerged from the undergrowth, limbs long and crooked, creeping towards them, so close they could smell the fresh earth on it, as it wordlessly stripped them of their clothes and disappeared into the fog leaving the two soldiers naked among the wheat grass, feeling a certain malaise, neither well nor poorly, at ease in their discontent, seeing the world as it always had been, to them, but with a concentration previously inaccessible, noticing, for example, that which they had until then taken for granted but never given thought to—the single grains growing on the grass and how that grass eventually became bread or beer or the way each blade moved on its own but also as one with the whole field, that the wind, which couldn't really be said to have a beginning or an end, appeared to have just that and moved like a wall through the grass, this rolling invisible wave . . . feeling numb, physically, which was just as well, for the abscesses that had opened on their skin grew and became infected and their limbs rotted and fell off and lay festering in the dirt beside them, dismembered like some forgotten cadaver, green with moss and gangrene, and some time later they died, feeling only a little out of sorts. Which was not supposed to happen.

At a distance we'd pass for a peasant family—pregnant mother, the father and son, their cart of belongings and their only cow—but if anybody got closer, they'd see that the cart was full of whisky and the pregnant lady was made of metal. And full of whisky. But if two soldiers were accompanying it? Well, we could only hope that they'd believe we had confiscated it.

The uniforms didn't fit, of course. I had to cut off the bottom of my kilt and wrap it around me several times. Sugar's was too wee. Even worn below his hips it didn't reach his knees.

I laughed at him, told him he looked like a silly wee lassie. He tore it off and put his trews back on.

—Anyone asks, I'll kill them, he said.

—Or you could just say they got damaged and they didn't have your size.

—I'd prefer to kill them.

I went behind the curtain in the kitchen and held my father's hand until it was time to go. Then I kissed him on the cheek.

—Back soon, I said.

We waved to my mother. She had one hand on her belly, blew me a kiss with the other.

My grandfather was going to walk us some of the way, said there was some folk he used to trade with who might put us up for a night.

We followed the path along the cliff and looked out to sea at the boats coming in, my father's not among them. The land was steep and barren, beaten by the wind and killed by salt from the sea. Only rocks grew here.

Eleven wooden crosses for the navvy who died on the bridge were scattered across the hill. They weren't working at the time, just taking a shortcut back to camp after getting pished in town. Up the scaffolding.

They had done it so often they could've climbed to the top in their sleep.

The path turned into a bog and we moved slowly. You'd climb upon a huge unseen rock with one foot and fall waist deep into a quagmire with the other. Even on the cart the old man didn't fare much better, feeling every bump as he held on with his arms wrapped around the metal lady sitting up front, listening to the sound of his baby slosh inside her distended belly. The cow, laden with bottles and jars and flasks hidden in blankets, did not seem to care that it struggled neck-deep in mud.

—Surely it would have been easier to kill the coo first.

—Nobody'd buy a deid coo, Heifer.

She was collecting eggs from the coop outside her home when she saw us, still a considerable distance away. When my grandfather waved the woman disappeared into her house.

—Hmmph, he said, surprised.

—Rude, I said.

Then we saw the woman beckon to us from her doorway to invite us in. She had arranged some stools around a small table and gestured for us take one while she folded a cloth around some coffee beans, ground them with a rolling pin and poured them into a pot of hot water that hung above the fire.

Her home was a single room with a sleeping area made private by a drape of tartan. Windows had been cut out of the stone but the glass was nailed in place and couldn't be opened.

She handed each of us a steaming mug of coffee and offered milk from a jug she placed on the table. She cradled her own cup in both hands, plaid shawl pulled around her shoulders as though she was seeking comfort from the cold, though it was stiflingly hot inside.

Her story came in whispery bursts between long silences, which my grandfather translated for me and Sugar, also in a whisper. All the while the woman stared into her cup.

Her husband was away selling their few pigs, my grandfather said. They'd had more. Once. Sheep as well and more than the single dairy cow they kept now but the landlord kept raising the rent and, having built the home themselves, planted their own crops, tended to their own livestock, milked the cows and slaughtered the pigs, and only traded what they didn't need themselves with a neighbour, had only just managed to keep ahead of it but now—she waved a hand dismissively—now it had been raised five-fold in the last three years alone.

She looked sorrowful. Her daughter was married and lived with her husband on one of the islands and her son had been killed fighting the French.

We rolled out our blankets on the dirt floor. The woman sat in her chair by the window all night, only moving to roll another cigarette. Though my body ached and begged for sleep, I could not. I imagined I was my father, so close to death all he could do was sleep, which sometimes helped, but didn't this time. I don't recall ever sleeping since, only these bits I don't remember. I am not embarrassed to admit that I was scared of this woman and suspected that she was a witch.

But I must have fallen asleep. I woke during the night to a man looming over me, babbling in some tongue not even my grandfather knew. The man's hair was long and matted tangles of locks draped down his chest and back, which were bare beneath the heavy fur he wore over his shoulders.

He turned to the woman and made this guttural sound whilst pointing at the fire, which was barely smouldering. Then he took the woman by the shoulder and pulled her up from the chair so she stood in front of the fire and pointed again, jabbering and nodding his head like an infant trying to make itself understood.

The woman finished rolling a cigarette and lit it. Then she collected some wood from outside and balanced it upon the hearth. She doused it with fat from a pan, which took light instantaneously. Only then did I notice the other man skulking behind the door. He, too, was barefoot and wore only a fur cloak but his hair and beard were not nearly as long as the other man's.

When the fire was going the older man took off his cloak to reveal that he was completely naked and urged his companion by the door to do the same. Tattoos and scars covered their bodies, visible even beneath the grey dirt or ash. They squatted by the fire, scrotes dangling in the dirt. Then they each took from their cloaks a human skull turned upside down and held it out to the woman who filled it with something from a clay urn. The younger one looked into his cup as he drank but the older one kept his eyes on the three of us.

—Best we get on our way, said my grandfather.

—No, the older man shook his head. No. You stay.

His voice was so raw it hurt to listen. Whatever it is inside a person that makes them speak, his was made of broken glass and bits of stone.

When he finished his drink he ordered the woman to refill it. Then offered some to us, his guests. He grinned absurdly. His teeth were white as bone but several of them were missing and the few left had been ground down to stumps. When we refused he shrugged and finished it himself. Then he wiped his hairy chin with the back of his hand and pissed into the skull. He offered it again. This time, when we refused, the man did not accept it. He shook his head violently and thrust the skull into our faces, one by one, till Sugar batted it away, spilling piss onto the floor.

—Get that fuckin thing out my face. He stood up.

The man went to throw the skull-cup at Sugar but feinted and drew back—that maniacal grin again—and drank from it with his pinky raised. Then he turned and squatted and shat into the skull.

My grandfather hauled me up and pushed me towards the door.

—Keep going, lass. Dinnae stop.

When I looked back I could see the woman watching from outside her house. She was still standing there when the path took us behind some trees and she was hidden.

My grandfather left us soon after that.

—I'm not going to be much use to you from here, he said. This is a changed place. Better without an old man like me holding you back.

To Sugar he said, See she's alright, and Sugar nodded. Then he gripped my shoulder, as affection, encouragement, and to steady himself, all at once.

I watched him trudge back towards the woman's house until Sugar shoved me onwards. Wouldn't see him again either.

After that we camped, either beneath Sugar's tent or under the stars, an empty sheepfold or a hastily abandoned croft if we were lucky. We kept off the main roads and paths but could not avoid the fort—fuckin useless thing that took so long to build there was no-one left to fight when it was finished. But it was occupied. For hours it loomed on the horizon, me and Sugar hoping that anybody who saw us from that distance would take us for simple peasants. A little closer and they would see two soldiers on foot leading a pregnant woman on a cart and think nothing of it. Just a crofter being escorted off the land.

Three soldiers came to greet us.

—Evening, said one of them.

—Evening, Sugar said, not in his usual accent.

The soldier looked Sugar up and down. I was expecting him to ask about his uniform—what happened to the rest of it—but they were not looking at the uniform. I had gotten used to his blue skin, the deformed tattoos, scars. Never occurred to me that anybody would be looking for somebody of his description.

I went to show them the hidden bottles, like we'd planned, make a point of displaying proudly the metal lady, point out the indents of a hammer, see where she'd been beaten into shape by hand and sealed with tar and filled with whisky, clothed and draped in scarves and a hat. I was to brag about how we became suspicious of her—how she remained completely still, even over rocky terrain, didn't so much as wipe her nose—and explain how it was a clever ruse but how we had been clever enough to see through it, that we had already sent word to the magistrate and were under strict orders to take the evidence to the city immediately and therefore had to beg their pardon and refuse their offer of hospitality for the evening, and then get as far from the place as possible, being prepared to ditch the booze, if necessary.

I never even got as far as pointing out the cart. Out the corner of my eye I saw Sugar punch one of the soldiers in the stomach. When I turned round he was stamping on the neck of the last one. The others were already dead—pulled apart by the jaw, face staved in. Their weapons lay beside them. Clean.

The rest of the journey went by in silence. I asked Sugar to tell me a story. He said he didn't know any.

More than four hundred and thirty locked in the hull. Wood already rotting from sea water decomposes further as human sweat, piss and shit seeps into it. Rainwater collects on the deck and percolates into the dungeon below where the rats burrow holes through the decaying wood like it's cheese.
He sits chained with his back against the hull like the others, staring.
Where do you think they're taking us? a man asks.
They're no takin us anywhere, says the one next to him, taking a rare break from gnawing at his flea-bitten arm with stumps of teeth. Didn't ye see? There's no mast on this boat.
Sure feels like we're goin somewhere.
S'just the tide, says the man between chews of his arm.

A BRIDGE JOINED THE OLD TOWN AND THE NEW, straddling a narrow street in permanent shadow, of pubs and inns, violence, vice, corruption, poverty . . . A place where folk went missing daily and turned up dead, sometimes, later, sometimes with bits of them missing. Hidden between the walls of the bridge were two streets, one above the other. Inside was a market where anything that could be sold could be bought, an entire person or just a bit of them, where pickpockets loitered and people who beat up pickpockets for sport waited and watched, where bodysnatchers preyed and where whores flaunted their wares and gave demonstrations, offered free samples—

—Oh yer a sailor are ye? Well ye can do me up the arse then!

She hoisted her tattered dress and turned, spreading her buttocks to display a smear of shite that reached all the way to between her shoulder blades. I was already struggling with my gag reflex from the profusion of smells trapped between the walls and vomited bile onto the stone floor.

The passageway was taller than it was wide, with

doorways leading off to smaller rooms beneath each arch of the bridge, to makeshift bars and brothels, dungeons and hotels and offices. Water dripped from stalactites taking shape in the curved ceiling. A glassy-eyed girl with a chain around her neck stood outside a heavy wooden door with a star scratched upon it, barred windows. When she caught me staring she smiled. I looked down, kept on pushing the cart.

Many a tempted eye followed but no-one dared steal from Sugar. In a place completely free of law and order, one could never be sure of the repercussions. In this way, the bridge regulated itself.

There was this old man standing with his back and the side of his face pressed flat against a wall. The backs of his feet and the palms of his hands were too, knuckles white, tendons taut. His grey hair and beard were long and matted and he had shat in his breeks. A younger man leaned casually in a doorway, smirking.

—What's wrong with him? I asked. Sugar went off to find someone.

—My son, ye mean? He thinks he is falling, said the younger man.

—Your son? But he's well old.

—It's all relative.

—He's a relative?

—No. *It* is all relative.

—It?

The man chuckled.

—Time, he said.

—You've lost me.

—I don't believe in it.

—You don't believe in time?

—Nope.

—And that stops you getting old?

—You're very clever, boy.

—How?

—It means you're intelligent.

—I mean, how does not believing in time stop you getting old?

—Time is a human construct.

—Eh?

—Ask yourself: why do we all stop what we're doing at night time and go to sleep?

—Because it's dark.

—Then light a candle. He shrugged. It's dark in here but we're all goin about our business just like we were out in the open. Some places in the world are dark all winter and light all summer.

—So you don't sleep?

—Of course I sleep. It's just that I don't have to.

—And that stops you from getting old?

—In a way, aye. If you stop counting days, months, years, by what unit do you measure yourself getting older?

—But won't your body just age the same?

—From wear and tear? That's only part of it. Are you aware of the three dimensions?

—The Father, the Son and the Holy Gho—

—No. The three dimensions. This . . .

He waved his arms around.

—Up, down, to, fro, left, right . . . The plane on which we exist is three-dimensional. Understand?

—No.

—You don't have to. It just is.

—Then, yes?

—You exist in these three dimensions because of

three bones in your ear, one for each axis. Up, down, left, right . . . ?

—To and fro.

—Exactly. So, say you take one of them away . . .

—One of the bones?

—Yes.

—You lose a dimension.

—You are very clever.

—Which did he lose?

—Out.

—Excuse me?

—This . . .

He held out his arms and turned around.

—It's all gone. But . . .

He stopped spinning.

—the problem is that now he is always falling. He only exists in two-dimensions: up and down, and side-to-side . . .

—Is that why he's always screaming?

—walls, floors, ceilings . . .

—If he can feel the floor how come he can't walk across it?

—I told you. Because he has no concept of outness. When he stands in the middle of a floor only the soles of his feet exist. The rest of him is lost. He has to slither on his front or on his back. He is but a drawing on a sheet of paper.

—What happened to the bone?

—Excuse me?

—In his ear.

—I have it.

—You have it. In your ear?

—Aye.

—What does it do?

—It lets me see time.

—Which you said didn't exist.

—Oh it does. Just not in the way you think it does. Time doesn't pass, it doesn't go anywhere. You can't control it. All you can do is record it.

—The fourth dimension.

—You are scared of time, like he is scared of anything that does not have a surface, because it is invisible to you. When you can see it, you can control it, move around inside it. When you can do this, measuring time is meaningless.

A butcher offered to buy the cow but we declined when all he could pay us with was sausages. Instead we sold it to a family living on the lowest level who took to it with knives, my feet wet with its blood.

We sold the whisky to one of the many gangs that formed, dissolved or were absorbed beneath the bridge. The men in the gang called it peat-reek even though it was not as smoky as that made out on the islands. The leader of the gang was expecting us, this stout, barrel-chested man, short but clearly capable of handling himself against all but the largest number of armed opponents. He sat on a cask in an alcove beneath one of the arches. The tobacco he smoked through a hand-carved pipe was sweet and pleasant, even over the smell of armpits and shite that otherwise filled the room. A silver cross dangled from one ear. His skin was copper and he hid his hair beneath a white cloth. He pulled at his side-whiskers when Sugar introduced us. Then he handed a purse of money to Sugar, who passed it to me. I didn't mean to snatch it but I was nervous and couldn't help it. Sugar put his hand on my back and steered me out the room.

—Have a look around, he said, closing the door.

I watched as they emptied our cart and carried our whisky off somewhere. I didn't look inside the purse. Couldn't count it anyway.

The empty cart was commandeered by a beggar missing his lower-half, who used his walking stick like a gondola oar to push it.

The girl was gone from outside the room with the star scratched on it but the door was open a crack. Light from a fire danced on the black walls but the colours were not ones I had ever seen a fire make before: greens and pinks and purples and blues, like a bruise . . . Without knowing it, I had taken steps in the direction of the door until I stood with my hand on its frame. The door opened and before me stood a woman of indeterminate age. Her skin was young, clean, her eyes wide and welcoming, innocent and wise. She seemed to look right through me, the way I could see right through her blouse. She stroked my chin and gently pushed and tilted my head back. I thought she was going to kiss me. I opened my mouth. Then she opened her other hand and blew a cloud of coloured dust into my face and I fell to the floor coughing, spluttering, eyes red and streaming—

I saw a man. Saw through his eyes the rough hands that held a lantern in one and a revolver in the other. I could feel the man's rage throbbing in his veins. Another man was lying on the ground between two metal rods running parallel as far as I could see in the dark. His head rested against a wooden board, one of many that seemed to hold the two rods together, like a ladder. He had one trembling hand held above his head in surrender, the other pressed ineffectively against a wound in his thigh from which black blood spurted. Behind us some people peered from a carriage, watching the shadow play, the men silhouetted by the glow of the lantern. More men—*his* men—piled loot by the trees. The cries and screams coming from the other carriages went unacknowledged.

How long have you been chasing me? the man rasped. I could feel his voice echo inside me.

The man on the ground trembled and his voice shook when he spoke, saying that he didn't know for sure but that it had been a long time. His hat lay beside him on the ground.

You're retired now, said the man with the gun. I kicked the hat.

The man nodded, blinking rapidly. His white moustache dripped red with the blood that poured from his nose.

They let you keep the uniform. The badge.

Left before they got a chance to ask.

Why me?

A man needs a hobby when he retires, he coughed. Black specks from his lungs dotted his face. Else you just curl up and die.

Before then.

After that girl went missing—

You know that wasn't me.

You were there. Not you, then one of your men.

It wasn't one my men. We don't do children.

He pushed back the hat on his head, made our shadow look like we were wearing a halo.

You're speaking for just yourself here? asked the man on the ground, planting his arms by his sides to prop himself upright.

They can choose to do or not do whatever they want. Consequences either way.

Then he sighed. I sighed.

This country was doing just fine before we came here. We filled it with the worst sort of people—entitled folk who'd run out of things back home to own and came out here to find more. And the ones they shat upon back home followed them over, bringing with them only a grudge and a righteous anger, come to take what they never had. We've regressed. The way I understand things is that so long as some people have nothing to start with, it's okay to make it so they have even less. That's progress. I don't want no part in it. And I don't think you do either.

The other man was bent over, clutching his bleeding thigh with both hands.

Let me ask you something, I heard myself saying, in a fight between two men, which one is the winner?

Through gritted teeth: The strongest.

The one who is most determined to win. Let's say one man attacks another. The man doing the attacking is in the wrong but his victim has a choice: to let himself be beaten or to fight back. But if the first man was so inclined as to attack another without provocation, he is not likely to let them win. Hell, he started the fight so he's damn well going to be the one that gets to finish it on his own two feet. So the victim, who has chosen to defend himself, has no choice but to continue fighting, otherwise he might as well have just lay down and taken the beating. But how do you win a fight against a man determined not to lose?

The other man said nothing. His face was in the gravel. He had let go of his thigh. The dried blood on his hands made them curl up like talons.

He has to be—you would say stronger, maybe, but I would say . . . worse. He has to be worse than the man who picked a fight with him. More violent, more evil. So he has fought back, knocked his assailant to the ground. Now what? If he lets the man go, the man is sure as shit going to get up and start swinging, and so the fight goes on. So he is going to have to put the boot in, end the fight for good. So the man who started the fight in the first place is in the wrong. Is evil. But for the good man to win, he has to be the most violent. Doesn't he? Make it so his attacker can't get back up. Does that make him a bad person?

The man on the ground turned stiffly and looked up squinting.

You can go to hell.

Suit yourself.

A fine powder puffed into the air and fell softly like black ash, returning to liquid when it hit the ground, red splashes on the rail, spots in the dirt. The shot ricocheted through the mountains and we listened to it until it passed. A woman leaning out of a carriage window covered her mouth with her hand then vanished inside.

I lowered the gun. Then I holstered it, pulled my hat down low over my brow and turned away from the body—

—staggering backwards—

—Watch yersel lad, said someone stepping over me.

I rubbed my eyes and scratched at my throat,

struggling to control my breathing. A hand on my collar pulled me up. The world warped like I was looking at it from underwater. Sugar's face, eyes swimming in his head, huge hands beckoning. I wrapped my arms around him.

—What happened to you, lass? he asked. The word *lass* sounded unusual in his strange accent, like I had never heard it before.

But when I tried to find the door to show him it was gone, just a brick wall in its place.

It was the screaming I heard first, when the raid must have been well underway and the arrests and beatings and the fighting back must have started and weapons were drawn. We were at the entrance. Shots were fired. People start running towards us into daylight. Sugar shoved me ahead of him. A woman sweeping piss and shit into the gutters screamed and ducked for cover. A bullet hit the stone behind me. Another came to a stop in the leg of a clerk on his way to work. The clerk sat down, knowing he should be pressing on the wound but not wanting to get the sleeves of his striped suit jacket all gosh-and-darn-it-all-to-bloody-hell bloody. Sugar lifted me onto a horse.

—I can't take somebody's horse.

—It's outside a butchers. It'll be sausages soon enough.

He smacked the horse on its side, told me to go.

Two soldiers clambered down the stairs behind me. One of them took aim but the other put his hand on the rifle.

—Ye'll more likely hit another pedestrian at this distance, he said, pointing with his thumb towards the bank clerk collapsed against the wall of the cemetery with his pocketwatch open in his hand, its chain leading to the mess of gore still bubbling from the bullet hole in his trousers. He would later lose the leg, his testicles and part of his penis—not to mention the three fingers one of the nurses who'd had to hold him down would lose whilst the doctor in the white smock stained brown with old blood hollered, Time me gentlemen! to the students observing him, Speed alone is the best defence against infection, as he leapt onto the gurney, cleaver held high—

—Ach, shite.

—Wait. There he goes.

The horse struggled on the cobbles but I pushed it onwards, not looking behind me. There was a snap like a branch breaking and the horse howled and threw me from the saddle. Its leg was bent beneath it. A yellow-white shard poked through the brown hair.

I'm sorry, I whispered. I'm sorry.

Hearing the slap of running feet echoing on the stone I tried to get up, walking my hands up the wall for support. I turned a corner and lurched down a set of stairs.

I closed one eye as the sky darkened, opening it only when the roads of the city formed a low roof over my head. Foul water ran through the constricted streets, clouded red where it met the puddle of blood beneath a disembowelled swine hanging from a hook. A group of children were splashing in the puddle.

—Sorry, mister, said one of them.

I shouldered passed the pig, sending it swinging.

Going deeper beneath the city, the people around me just shadows, an occasional face or body part flickering in the light of the few torches hung outside doorways, candles in the small rounded squares I assumed were windows. The air was thick and rank. The boots of the men following me echoed in the basement city.

An empty house lay open on a corner, deserted and unlit. I entered and closed the door behind me. I crouched beneath the window with my back to the wall, listening. The footsteps got louder then receded and eventually all I could hear was my heart beating, my shallow breaths. After a while my heartbeat slowed and I closed my eyes and focused on taking low slow breaths, in . . . and out, in . . . and out. Only when I was as calm as one could reasonably be in such a situation did I hear the other breathing, which, until now, had been more or less synchronised with my own, shallower, rattling and whistling like a bird's nest in a chimney, the quick, useless inhalations of somebody trying to suppress a sob and failing, whimpering in the dark.

Cowering by the foot of the box-bed was a young girl. Her face was white with cracked skin and she mewled in pain. Puss wept from broken sores. I pressed myself against the wall like I was trying to pass through it. The girl reached out a hand, the boils on the back of it rupturing. I scrambled to the door, the white face of the girl in my peripheral vision, more than just this shape in the dark, lingering like the shape of the sun behind your eyelids, and staggered back the way I had come.

I got lost near where the children splashed in the pig's blood. They were gone and so was the pig. I kept walking till I came out somewhere west of the city. The clouds of soot and the stench of human waste were gone, replaced by a grey sky that pissed sulphur onto fields of animal dung. Gone were the cobbled streets. Instead, a narrow dirt path followed a road of water.

I knew my brother was dead. Saw the clumps of his flesh fall to the floor when the lashes tore through him. Saw his ribs through the gouges in his back. Saw him swinging from the gallows like a burst bag of meat.

I tried to make myself feel better, believe that everything was okay and that he had been released and was probably on his way home right now and he would be there waiting on me when I got there, if I didn't meet him on the way . . .

I stopped walking and screamed till my lungs were empty. It was like I had been broken in some way, on the inside, and every part of me seemed to be turning towards it. I cried for my brother, for my failure to help him, and from the pain in my ankle.

—Excuse me, sir.

I opened my eyes. My ankle was dark blue with these red blotches dotted upon it. It had swelled up till it was wider than my calf.

—Excuse me, sir.

My hands were curled up like a cripple's and only when I noticed this did I realise that they hurt, though I couldn't untwist them.

—Excuse me, sir.

I looked up. A man leading a horse pulling a barge wanted passed. I considered asking for help but had nothing with which to pay. I would have offered to work but the boat was heading back to the city, so I stood aside for the man and the horse.

Are you alright, lad? the Captain calls out in a hoarse voice only a few feet away—just another outline of a body in the dark, the guards having grown fearful of providing light in case the volatile mix of human gases should ignite and explode. The only light was what could squeeze through the cracks in the ceiling or those rare and brief moments when the hatch was opened and some hard bread was thrown in.

There is a quiver to the Captain's voice. The can hear him shuffle towards him.

Shivering, the Captain asks for water.

You know I don't have any, he hisses and the Captain shuffles back to his spot next to what remains of the mast in the centre of the room and slumps against it with his shaking arms folded across his chest.

AS I VENTURED FURTHER FROM THE CITY GREAT fissures opened in the ground from which fire erupted. Black smoke engulfed me and the path was no longer visible. The water of the canal bubbled and buildings alongside it crumbled and disappeared into chasms below whilst their former occupants watched, huddled together on red hills of shale.

A circular wall enclosed a single tree on fire. I huddled behind the wall and prepared to die. When I woke the sky was that same combination of black smoke and red flame it was when I had closed my eyes. I didn't know if it was night or day.

After a time the smoke cleared but I still couldn't see for the trees. I could only hope I was still going west. I crossed a river with the water up to my armpits, grateful for the weight off my ankle, till I lost my footing on a rock that turned over when I stood on it and was nearly washed away. At the other side I hauled myself onto the embankment using the roots of a tree soon to be taken by the water and swallowed a mouthful of midges. I tried to spit but my mouth was dry and a noodle of saliva dangled from my chin and almost reached the ground before I wiped it away. I pulled myself to the top of the slope using branches and small trees and weeds and looked around to get my bearings. Ahead lay endless fields but that way was south. I needed to go north but in that direction was the river I had just crossed and the vast unknowingness of a forest. Keeping the treeline to my right I continued west till I joined up with the canal and followed it till it began to curve northwards through more red hills of loose stone that threatened to slip and bury everything beneath them.

When night fell I left the path and climbed one of the red hills. They were not high but it took longer than expected. With every step I took I sank and was carried further down the hill than where I was when I took it. In the end I resorted to crawling, using the few shrubs that sprouted through the stones to assist, quickly letting go of each one when I plucked their shallow roots from the hillside and moving onto the next.

At the top I sat with my swollen ankle stretched out in front of me, watching the canal, the smear of sky barely making it through the red hills that erupted from the ground in every direction. I could see the way the river cut the land in two, like the part of it I was sitting on had been severed from the other side and the sky behind the world could be seen in the gulf between.

The sky was dark but the pink dust in the air stopped it from going out completely. I lay on my back and stared at the night sky like I did back home during the summer, when I would fall asleep and my brother would have to come find me in the morning and I would wake with a mouthful of desiccated midges.

He might have slept but the difference between waking and sleeping is indistinguishable to him now. Awake, he sits staring into darkness and when he sleeps he dreams of the same, chained—like one of <u>them</u>—in the hull of a rotting ship bobbing in the water, lulling him to sleep—no easy feat when you're starving to death and what little fluids you do imbibe are expelled ten-fold from your arsehole minutes later.

Boy, whispers the Captain. Do you have any water?

He can just about make out the Captain in the dark, scratching and pulling at his dirty wet tunic, clawing at his chest and stomach and arms.

You know I don't, he rasps in reply and closes his eyes again.

He dreams that he has been shot and that the wound is festering and gangrenous. He is soaked with sweat and too hot and too cold and he digs his fingers into the bullet wound and licks the sticky fluid from them with a parched tongue—

I HAD BEEN CLAWING MY SKIN IN MY SLEEP AND WAS bleeding from cuts in my hands and arms. The dust had settled so I could see the red metal behemoth emerging from the river. If anybody was looking for me—and I had to assume they were—they would likely retrace the route I took to get to the city. I considered venturing to the river, stealing a boat and making my way back up the east coast but decided it was too dangerous. I had to continue west. If I was going to go by boat then at least the west coast would take me home. I couldn't recognise my own country on a map but I knew that much. Of course, there was the risk of pirates, of being taken captive and sold as white gold or forced to marry and give birth to a litter of barbarians. I decided that I would deal with that if I ever reached the coast.

I attempted to climb down the red hill carefully but quickly realised it was easier to let the scree move under me, let it carry me, and I reached the bottom in no time. My ankle by now was solid and painless and I took this to be a good thing.

Then a buzzing came from the clouds, from some

flock of animals I couldn't see, but the noise grew too loud. An explosion shook the ground and I fell, unable to tell what it was that caused it. I saw a plume of water rise from the river. There was another explosion, further away this time, and when I looked back I saw a trail of black smoke and this winged creature, far bigger than any bird I had ever seen before, but in an instant it was away.

I came to a set of steps that led from the canal up to the stone bridge that crossed it. The bridge was crowded with carts and cows and pigs and horses and dogs that scurried between the legs of men hauling barrows, woman and children on their way to work in the mines.

I got caught taking a handful of oats from a horse's feeding bag.

—What de ye think yer daein lad?

Two men appeared and the driver of the cart pointed at me. I darted through the crowd and ran till I was out of breath, between buildings, through gardens, over fences and walls and through hedgerows until I couldn't go on anymore and fell to the ground clutching my stomach and dry-heaving. I hadn't collapsed but, rather, had tripped on a plank of wood and had just missed clattering my head off another one a few feet away. More planks were laid on the ground at equal distances in both directions, joined together by two metal rails, like a ladder. I remembered my dream, what I thought at the time was a dream or a hallucination, from the dust the woman beneath the bridge blew in my face. I saw the planks and the rails and the man resting his head against them, bleeding, the gun in my hand and the way his face collapsed in on itself when the bullet went through a hole in the bridge of his nose that wasn't there before and how his head seemed to pop and vomit pink onto the tracks, and my hands shook. I was hungry.

I followed the tracks through the trees and came to a squat stone building with a tall chimney. I smelled bread. A grey road, flatter than any I had seen before, led to other buildings, a village. I thought it wise to keep away from the larger ones, several of which dotted the low hills, poking through gaps in the trees. I saw a church spire and considered making my way to it and hadn't decided when I felt a hand on my shoulder and, when I touched it to push it away, noticed with horror that it was not like any hand I had ever felt before, but cold and hard. I turned and screamed at the man in white, at his shiny, rigid, immobile face. I pushed him away so hard I fell over but my hands and legs were trembling and I couldn't get up.

The man walked towards me. He had his hands in the air and I could see now that one of them, though flesh-coloured, was smooth and solid like the mask that clung to his face. That *was* his face. I sat panting on the ground, ready to move if he came too close. But he stayed where he was, hands still above his head. He said something but I could not hear it clearly.

—What? I said.

The same muffled sound again. I thought he said, I'm not going to hurt you. I didn't believe him.

—Are you lost?

This was clearer. He was making an effort to be understood.

I could see one eye behind a slit in the mask but

couldn't find a slit for the other. He spoke through a series of square holes where a mouth would be. There weren't any nose holes. The mask was flat where his nose should be. I could hear him breathing.

—You don't look well, he said.

—Speak for yourself.

The man made a gesture that wasn't quite a shrug, just the gist of one.

—What are you? I asked, standing up.

—Now there's a question I've never been asked before.

I could understand him clearly now. Maybe it wasn't him at all; maybe I just wasn't used to people conversing with me.

—Where I'm from, people are normally known as a who, not a what.

—Where are you from? Are you from . . . I pointed at the sky.

—Space? Jesus, lad. You really are lost aren't you?

It was my turn to shrug but I didn't have the energy. He got the general idea.

—Are you hungry?

I could taste acid in my mouth, my body trying to dissolve and eat itself.

—Let me get you something.

He took me to a low building painted white. Inside, shelves of bread and labelled jars of coloured pebbles and cylinders of metal lined the walls. The man without a face reached into a cabinet and brought out a bag made of brown paper and put several items in it: a loaf of bread, cheese and a glass bottle of milk.

—I'm going to need that bottle back, he said. But, if

I was to guess, I'd say you had no intention of sticking around.

He held out the bag.

—I'll tell them it broke, he said.

If he had a mouth I imagined it was smiling. I took the bag, thanked him and left.

When I had got as far from the village as I could I stopped behind a wall to eat, finishing everything. I almost decided against returning the bottle but reasoned that it was the right thing to do and ran back to the white building and left the empty bottle in a wooden box by the door. Inside the box was another loaf of bread. I put it inside the paper bag and set off.

The man nearest him jabs him in the ribs with his elbows. His eyes sting like the lids are spreading sand on the surface. Sweat runs from the man's brow and drips onto his chest, bare from having torn his shirt open, scratched and bleeding from where he has clawed at his flesh with dirty fingernails, a webbed rash growing across his torso, disappearing beneath his clothes and reappearing on his forearms, stretching towards his trembling fingers—

DAYS LATER I CAME TO A SMALL TOWN. THOUGH wary of being caught, I checked each home for food, and, although their furniture remained, and books and a few ornaments too, no-one came back, not even after night had fallen. One or two chickens roamed but I was too exhausted to catch one, never mind pluck it and cook it. Instead I chewed on dried oats I found in a barn.

I woke to the sound of sheep. They had made their way towards the warmth of my fire during the night, an entire herd, it seemed, in the only room of the tiny cottage I had chosen to sleep in. There were more of them outside, chewing the grass, wandering aimlessly between the deserted buildings.

At the coast I considered stowing aboard a ship but thought better of it and hung back until anybody who had noticed me forgot about it. I stole a fish from a cart, stuffed it down my shirt and ran. I hid in a boathouse and wondered how to go about cooking it. Ended up eating it raw, tearing the piss-flavoured flesh from the spine, teeth slipping on the slimy skin, prolonging the misery, retching and bringing up every other mouthful, which I was careful to choke back down lest the whole ordeal become a waste of time. I dared not move, expecting I would soon be shitting myself inside-out, but was pleasantly surprised to discover that I was fine. Felt good, in fact.

When it got dark I started north, winding my way through trees that gave way to stone, then to moss. The ground beneath me sank when I stood on it and sprang back into place behind me. When I slept on it, it was like pillows. I took to sleeping during the day and walking when the sun dipped behind the horizon, its glare obscuring me from anybody who might have been watching.

The ground grew steeper and I covered less of it each night, though the sky stayed dark for longer. I drank from streams and sometimes puddles, straining dirty water through an even dirtier shirt. Once I drank from a burn only to find a rotting sheep's carcass half-submerged upstream. For a couple of days afterwards you could have supped my shite from a spoon. When the snow started I ate it by the handful.

I heard them before I saw them. Ghosts. Their voices carried by the wind through the valleys. There was nowhere to hide, no trees, not even a clump of heather. I considered burying myself in the snow but, while the notion of dying in my sleep appealed to me, I decided against it. Not when I had made it this far. I'll be home soon, I told myself.

I climbed down to the beach hoping to find a cave or an overhang I could crawl into but there was none. So I kept walking, spent the night in a dwelling of reasonable condition, abandoned in a hurry, on a tiny island I could wade out to, the water at its deepest just up to my middle. The island was mostly loch, protected from the sea by hand-hewn cliff walls, its surface flat as glass, purple at the bottom, where I could see clearly the shovels and picks and barrows and piles of flat rock, as if left there for the next day while the men who they belonged to went home for their tea.

I watched from the doorway the flickering torchlight and elongated shadows of the folk on the shore, walking the corpse road.

The next morning, before it was light, I walked to the other side of the island. The black water merged with the grey sky. The edge of the world. I found a rowboat half-sunk in the crude bay but didn't have the strength to dig it out.

The black sea thrashed at the coast. The world by now had turned to shades of grey. Snow that fell from the charcoal sky melted into the dirt and froze again, rocks sticking out here and there like stumps of teeth in rotten gums, or gravestones. I didn't notice the ash at first, not till it came down like burnt snow and didn't melt when it landed on me. By then I could smell it—the foul, acrid stench of burning in the air.

A blanket of dust scattered by the wind and patches of charred earth cut through borders of ice. I felt in my pocket for the pouch of tobacco I had procured for the old woman as I walked in silence past the square of ash and stone that was once her house, the burnt and blackened trees nearby that were still standing holding vigil over the remains. Fresh snow covered the tracks of whoever did this. A single purple flower grew from between a crack in a rock untouched by the blaze and I kicked the unopened bud from its stem with my bare feet and moved on.

The hermit had been following me for some time. I thought he was walking the corpse road, stuck in a separate loop from the others. When I turned to look he made no attempt to hide, just stood there in the empty land as though the dried moss and dirt that clung to him made him invisible. I would call to him and he would remain silent. Whenever I stopped, he would stop as well. I didn't have it in me to turn back and confront him. Then one morning, when I had settled on the grass to sleep, he came crawling towards me and squatted by the fire. He planted his walking staff into the ground before him and held onto it like it was keeping him from toppling over. Even up close it was impossible to see where the ground ended and his skin began—foliage sprouted from pores, curls of dry leaves, green-brown flecks of moss that fell from him when he spoke, one eye hidden, the other made of stone . . .

—Lo there, I said.

His voice rustled like a bag of dead leaves. He spoke for some time so I assumed he was telling a story.

When he finished I offered him some bread but when he went to take it his arm broke off at the elbow and crumbled like charcoal, bicep twitching. His mouth moved like it was chewing, straw beard undulating when he swallowed, but the bread had fallen to the ground. In the morning only a clump of mulch remained, perched on the stone on which he had sat. I tasted dirt and rust in my mouth, the stench of ammonia in my nostrils, and spat.

Captain, he rasps, slowly pulling himself up by his chains into a crouching position. Captain.
He climbs up the wall till he stands as upright as he can manage, steadying himself against the rocking of the ship. He shouts again, louder, but his voice is drowned out by the sea smashing against the hull and the rain lashing the deck above. Gripping the chain, he takes a slow careful step, like that of a drunk, avoiding the sprawling figure of the man opposite, then another, in the direction of the Captain. After three steps he has reached the end of his length of chain but is able to reach his friend.
Captain, he shouts, hoarse, shaking him by the shoulder.
The Captain opens one eye, shielding his face with his hand as though it is too bright down there in the pitch black. His head lolls.
Water, he says.
You know I don't have any.
The Captain closes his eyes and his head slumps into his chest. He opens one eye again, squints, lets his dry tongue do some laps round his mouth, which hangs open. A dry string of spit stretches across his desiccated lips like the teeth of some deep sea fish.
The ship lurches and he almost falls, clutching at the chain to keep himself upright. The hatch opens briefly, the illumination allowing just enough time to see the rash that covers the Captain's face.
Captain, he shouts but the Captain doesn't respond. He tugs at the Captain's shirt collar but the Captain just flaps his hand and returns it to his lap and picks at the rotten sore on the back of it with the other.

IN THE FIRE PITS THAT DOTTED THE LANDSCAPE I kicked through the ashes to see what had been burnt and was sickened but not surprised at the odd limb or other body parts, jawbones and whathaveyou that hadn't been consumed by the fire before it died. I had no intention of stopping anywhere near this place but it never ended.

Eventually I came to a building I recognised: the kirk. It was missing its roof and two walls but still had the altar, like it was yet to be finished.

I minded when the chief told us we were building a new one, that we were to follow a new religion—

—A different god, like? someone asked.

—No, it's the same god, said the chief.

—But in a different kirk.

—Aye.

—For the same god.

—Aye.

—So, God wants two kirks, aye?

—How come?

—Because it's a different religion. It'd be

sacrilegious to worship a new religion in the old kirk.

But wood was scarce and it was hard work digging and transporting stone, especially when we weren't allowed to work a Sunday and we couldn't very well turn down paid work on the canal to build something for free, and so for six days the men carried stone from this old kirk to build the new one. It was never finished.

When I got to the kirk and saw what was already there I was forced to keep moving. His beard was longer and his locks reached the floor. He sat cross-legged on a body. He smiled when he saw me and beckoned for me to sit down but I remained where the door used to be. He stood up, which was when I saw that the body was the old woman. He took me by the arm and made me sit down on a stone he moved into place before the small fire. He crouched down to blow on the coals and his blue balls slopped between his thighs like offal. He offered me a drink but I declined, though I was parched. My tongue burned raw from the snow.

The man returned to his corpse and sat on it cross-legged, grinning. Then he drank deeply from the upturned skull he clasped in both hands. I must have gone to sleep because when I opened my eyes he had prepared a meal.

He lifted a skewer of meat from the fire.

I ate it gratefully. It was charred on the outside and bled when I bit into the centre but was otherwise tender and well-seasoned with saltwater.

I nodded thanks, said it was good.

The man seemed pleased and rewarded himself with another drink from the skull, which by now was starting to seem like an acceptable drinking vessel. He offered me a drink and this time I accepted, closing my eyes as I took the skull in my hands and sipped. The alcohol stung my nostrils as my nose dipped into the skull. The liquid was sweet and thick but burned my throat unexpectedly and my tonsils ached when I swallowed. I grimaced but the man seemed pleased.

—I made you something, he said, and took from behind the altar a necklace, or head-dress, I wasn't sure, as it got tangled in my hair when he tried to put in on me. It appeared to be made of fishing line and something hard, like twigs or seashells. As he tried to untangle it from my hair bits of it came apart and dropped into my lap. I picked up a piece and held it up to the light to see what it was, saw the row of dentures. I felt for the rest of the decorations embedded in my knotted hair and tried to take it off, gripping my hair in one hand and tearing out the decoration with the other.

—What are you doing? he shouted, holding my wrists.

—Get off me! I shouted. Let go!

He pushed me back against the wall of the kirk. Meat-breath steamed from between his yellowed teeth. Ash and blood streaked his face. I thrust my knee hard into his balls and he dropped to the floor. He didn't appear to find the experience unpleasant and tugged on his cock till it grew long. Then he lay down on his back and pissed on his stomach. I stopped running only when the light from the kirk had disappeared in the dark to stick my fingers down my throat and bring up whatever it was he fed me.

Swaying with the spastic lurches of the ship, he looks around, peers at the hunched shadows in the dark, scratching, shivering, or unresponsive. Voices overhead, footsteps, thuds indistinguishable from the rattle of the heavy rain on the deck. The sounds of panic: shouting, screaming . . . A rumbling from the sky followed shortly by a flash, showing him, if only for a second, that which afflicts his comrades down there in their dungeon. Puss squeezes through open sores like yellow worms; flesh putrefies and falls in stinking clumps from men who otherwise appear to be suffering only the after-effects of a night's heavy drinking.
Sugar begins to panic.

I SAW IT ON THE CREST OF THE HILL, LONG BEFORE I was close enough to make out who it was hanging from the tree, his dumb eyes open, watching me approach. His neck was broken and the force of the drop that did it had been enough to push more of the poor soul's brain through the scabbed-over hole in the top of his skull, dried and black like dead worms. The mouth hinged open, slack, the way it had in life, the useless tongue no longer lapping at the palette, clothes loose on skin stretched taught over bones like a pelt being cured.

Three more bodies hung upside down from the bridge. All were missing limbs, one of them a head. There had been a fourth, as evidenced by a rope that twirled in the wind, who had been hung by the neck but the head had popped off when its owner had been pushed from the top of the aqueduct and both head and body fell into the street and landed with a sticky thud that splintered the planks of the new wooden road that ran through the town.

In the time I'd been away, Badwater had undergone a transformation, one that was still taking place, that in fact would never stop. The canal would continue being built and wouldn't be finished till long after it was needed, behind schedule and several times over budget, seldom used before it would fall into disrepair and be abandoned, then refurbished and reopened years later as a tourist attraction to satisfy a nostalgia for a narrative that never existed, made obsolete before it was even complete by the railway, then the roads and later the cars that brought visitors who would stand on the crags and take photographs of where the loch opened into the sea, where flat stones on the ground delineated walls of cramped dwellings and a sign explained a little about the Clearances next to a hand-drawn map of what someone surmised the shanty town must've looked like, minus about two-thirds of the houses . . . Just ruins to be gawped at by tourists who feel nothing but the cold through their recycled plastic water-bottle sweatshirts.

The road had been paved with wood too slippery to walk on so I trod through the snow and frozen dirt alongside it. The town was busier than I had ever seen it. Rich folks, piss-drinkers from the south, landowners, businessmen, slavers and traders, relished the sights of the corpses, the violent, savage customs, safe in their hotel rooms. It was not their place to intervene, though they could—*and should*, they would argue—criticise, amongst themselves only, for now, content to write or sketch it in their journals, later to be published in magazines and embellished in taverns, their tales of the Neanderthals of the north at the end of the world. The workers just ignored them, got on with digging the canal or building the bridge, more of them now, folk who had come just for the work, since the canal had fallen even further behind schedule and most of the original workers had been bundled onto ships and sold to plantations or relegated to the ramshackle huts that balanced on the narrow ledge of rock between the sea and the loch, or dead. Those with any sense spent the time they weren't working staggering between the inns, bakeries and betting shops. Might as well have paved the streets with their spew.

The loch had frozen over and the aqueduct was no closer to being finished than when I had last seen it. It appeared to have been abandoned. The black faces of sheep, otherwise invisible in the snow, freckled the fields in their hundreds and there was no trace of the crofts that used to be there.

But as I trudged around the loch I soon saw the ruins of them, the scorched brick, furniture and other belongings protruding from the snow like shrapnel.

Out on the thin stretch of rock that divided the loch and the sea, where once only a few desperate souls had lived, the rock itself was no longer visible, hidden by the shanty town that covered it, built with whatever materials were to hand—an upturned rowboat or a salvaged door leant against the outside wall of an accommodating neighbour, some of them just holes dug into the ground as shelter against the wind until something more permanent could be cobbled together. Entire families would burrow into the dirt, in tunnels like ant colonies or burial chambers. When the explosions started the soil in the tunnels would drop in one great lump, not as a shower of dirt and stone like you'd imagine, slowly suffocating you as the dirt takes the place of the air, but which you could escape from if you hurried, just this single slab that flattens you, squeezing your insides through burst fingertips in an instant.

Welcome to Badbae. A vile country, to be sure.

I made my way along the tops of the cliffs, away from Badwater, and down the rough-hewn steps to the cave where my brother made whisky, empty but for a few feet of water from where the loch leaked in through a crack in the roof. On my way back I heard a voice and looked up to see a man steadying himself on a rock, clutching a green bottle. I was out of breath by the time I reached him. The man was walking away.

—Wait, I shouted. What did you say?

—What? the man said without stopping.

—You said something to me. When I was down in the cave.

—What were you doing down there?

—I was looking for someone.

—That's what I said. He stopped.

—Excuse me?

—That's what I said. I said, What are you doing down there?

—I just told you, I said. Looking for someone.

—That's what I said.

The man took a drink from the bottle. Then he held it out in front of him, away from me, and it took me a moment to realise that he was offering me a drink. I took the bottle, took a swig.

—That Lawdun boy sure makes good whisky.

I had not really expected to find him here but, still, I held in my head, during the long walk home, the whole way, this image of him sitting in our doorway waiting for me, and I would see him and run to him—

—*Made* good whisky, I should say. Then the blind man made the sign of the cross.

—What do you know?

He's dead, lad. They all are.

They had come from the water pulling their rowboats behind them onto the sand, unheard over the crashing of the sea against the rocks, made their way through each of the primitive huts and took what valuables they could find, though there were not many—people barely coping have little use for trinkets. Moving swiftly in bare feet through the long grass they came to the camp upon the hill where the navvy slept and set their tents ablaze, watching as they woke, fumbling with their sleeping sacks, crawling through the burning canvas to be marched at gunpoint to the shore. Those who were not able to march were killed on the spot and those who fought back were commended for their courage and beaten and, if they could, made to walk or crawl to the boats waiting for them on the beach, ashamed and unable to look in the eyes of the women and children who stood alongside them, who they had failed to keep safe.

My father, unable to move, to defend his home against the raid, had watched from his sickbed as the invaders wrestled my mother to the floor, kicking and clawing and biting at the two men it took to hold her down, unable to shout or reach a useless hand out for my mother to squeeze when they lifted her skirts and saw she was with child and pulled her to her feet by her hair, which came away from her scalp in a clump, sending the man who pulled it flying backwards into his companion, who took a knife from his belt and thrust it into my mother's belly repeatedly while she clawed at his face, screaming silently as the blood of her baby spilled from her mouth. Then he walked her backwards with the knife in her and lifted her off her feet, let her fall onto my father's bed, her head rolling to one side, the two of them looking into each other's eyes for the last time when they cut my father's throat.

—What happened to the son?

—Which one? One got taken to Edinburgh and the other went to bring him back. The first one was hanged. The other one, I don't know.

—And the grandfather?

The blind man shrugged, offered me another drink, which I declined. Then he shrugged again, raised the bottle in a half-hearted toast, took a drink, and wiped his mouth on the back of his hand and left me standing alone at the edge of the cliff.

I had been there when my brother was caught. I'd heard the minister's warning, saw him gallop towards the cliff on his horse, shouting, The Philistines be upon thee, Samson, his bible clutched against his chest with one hand, the horse's reins in the other.

We had a routine for when the excisemen came. Canteens were hidden and bottles were buried, copper stills dismantled and disguised amongst fishing gear. Pouches of gruit were emptied into wort boiling in the kale yard and passed off as ale instead of being distilled into whisky.

A plume of smoke rose from the sea and I ran towards it. At the cliffs the path wound down, narrow and stepped. I could barely see the shale of the beach below from the billowing smoke. I called out to my brother. Up on the road, looking my way, were the excisemen. Ahead of them was the minister.

I unhitched my brother's horse from the post by the steps and slapped it, sent it on its way along the cliffs. Then I started down the steps.

Shielding my eyes, I entered the smoky cave and found him emptying a bucket of seawater onto the hot coals beneath the still.

—They're here. We need to go.

I couldn't breathe.

My brother ran to the beach, to a rowing boat turned upside down.

—What are you doing?

He gripped one edge of the boat and squatted to lift it. Gritting his teeth he said, Get under.

I didn't know what to do.

—Now!

So I did what he said, expecting him to follow me under, worrying about whether we would be safe beneath the only boat on a beach with just the one way out. But when he didn't join me I lay on my back and braced my legs against the wooden boards and lifted the boat, turning my head to see, through the gap between it and the sand, my brother dismantling the still. The coals were still smouldering as he took it apart with just the cuffs of his shirt pulled over his hands to protect them. I could see the pain on his face but he stayed quiet.

—Leave it, there's no time, I whispered.

I saw the excisemen on the bottom steps.

My brother grabbed what he could, bottles under his arms, in his hands.

—Leave them. There's no time, I cried, tears streaming down my cheeks. Then my legs quivered and gave way and I dropped the boat. When I had the strength to lift it again I saw my brother on his knees facing the excisemen. His hands were tied behind his back and his head swung low. Blood ran from his ruined face and he glowered at the soldiers ransacking our distillery. Soon, an impressive collection of bottles, canteens, pouches, barrels and repurposed milk urns built up on the beach, and, with each addition, the excisemen only looked more pleased. When it was finished they congratulated one another with a pat on the back and a shake of the hands.

Then they found me hiding beneath the boat.

The chief and the gaoler had stood outside my cage. Sellar skulked by the door. The excisemen were gone. So was my brother. In the cell next to me was Sugar.

—Hang her till she's nearly dead, Sellar had said.

—Nearly deid? said the gaoler.

—Aye, said the chief.

—But how'll I know when that is?

—When you think she's nearly dead, bring her down, said Sellar.

—I'm no sure I'll be able to tell. Some folk go quicker than others, sometimes right away. Like if their neck was to snap—

—Don't snap her neck. No drop. Sellar shook his head.

—So I've just to hang her for a wee bit.

—Exactly. Until she's nearly dead.

—That's the thing, see. There's no way I can know when that will be. It's no an exact science—

—For fuck sake, said the chief.

—I could lash him if you like.

—Lash a girl?

—So hanging her's alright but no lashin?

—Fine. Lashes.

—Till she's nearly deid.

—Fuck sake man, no. She'd have no skin left. Just give her a few.

—Three lashes.

—Three hundred.

—Three hundred! On a wee lassie? The last hunner'n'fifty'd be me whipping the post she's tied to.

—In the name of the wee man. The chief groaned, rubbed his brow in exasperation. Use your common sense—

He stopped, opened his eyes, saw the joy on Sellar's face, leaning forward, rubbing his hands together like he was preparing for a wank. The thought of me being lashed to near-death (and likely to die from the wounds later) clearly excited him.

—What about her old man? asked the chief.

—Auld Lawdun?

—Naw, Big Lawdun.

—Wee Lawdun?

—His father. *Her* father.

—I suppose you could say he's as near-deid as ye could get, after the beating those soldiers gave him. Do you want me to use him as an example like?

—Whit?

—For the girl. I could use her faither as an example of near-deid so that when she gets into a similar state I'll know when to stop.

The chief shook his head.

—Just, he took a long breath, Give her ten and let her go.

I was hunched in the corner, arms draped across my knees, head bowed, lank hair hanging across my swollen face. Red veins crossed my pink eyes; my chin a glaze of bloody snotters.

The gaoler jerked his head in the direction of out.

—Away ye go, lass.

I stood up shakily and, with little more than a glance in the direction of the man at the door of the cage, hurried home.

Smoke billowed out when I opened the door. My mother was crouching at the hearth, poking at the smouldering peat while rain poured in through the chimney. I wrapped my arms around her. She turned to cradle her wee girl in her arms.

—It's going to be alright, she said, hugging me to her breast. Then she spat on her sleeve and gently wiped the blood and tears from my cheeks.

When we had both finished she told me we were moving. Then she chewed her lips and nodded a few times as if she was confirming this with herself.

—How? I asked. Cause of what happened?

My mother sighed.

—Just . . . We're no goin far. Just up to Badbae.

—For the fishing?

My gaze drifted towards the curtain, behind which my father was waiting to recover or to die.

—Aye, my mother smiled, for the fishing.

I tried to believe her. She pulled me close, only then noticing that the wetness of the shirt on my back, what she thought was rain, had dried sticky on her fingers. She lifted me off her knee and turned me around and saw the blood seeping through. I muttered a few words of reassurance. Then I collapsed to the floor.

I kicked away the snow.

All that was left of our home was a burnt square and some blackened stones. Behind me the unfinished aqueduct cut through the valley and loomed over Badwater; the walls of the reservoir a black line on the horizon separating the ashen hills from the grey sky.

Water.
You know I don't have any.
Water.
You know I don't have any.
He sits with his back against the hull, feeling the gentle listing of the boat one way, followed by the jagged lurch of it the other. He feels a rush of water against his face and opens his eyes. A wooden shard protrudes from the eye of the man chained opposite him. Bloated corpses bob in the water alongside faeces, bits of wood, scraps of bread, clothing, and rats both dead and alive. Survivors stand in waist-deep water tugging at the chains which bind them to this watery hell, crying for help, whilst others claw at themselves, sweating and mumbling deliriously in a fever whilst the water pulls on their straggly beards.

THE INNKEEPER SHOVELLED THE SNOW THAT HAD fallen during the night from the entrance to the hotel, stopping only to converse for a moment with the two lads repairing the hole in the road where, the night before, a man had been stabbed and the blood from his wound had froze him to the ground. They tried for a while to chip away at the frozen blood with a chisel, then a pick-axe, before deciding just to cut out that section of the wooden road and carry it away with the dead man upon it like an offering.

—Whisky, said Sugar to the bartender.

—I can't tempt you with ale? The bartender smirked.

—Whisky will do fine. Something tells me not to trust your ale.

He nodded at Young, at a table by himself, grown dishevelled, disinterested in living since his beloved Elizabeth's mercury-filled teeth exploded in her gums, leaving her mouth a sagging mess of scar tissue and dangling sinew that, even when pinned and sewn into place by the best doctors in Edinburgh and London, one of whom patched her up as a last resort with cheeks cut from a fresh cadaver, which became infected and had to be cut away along with even more of her own rotting face, never healed, and she killed herself with the first dose of laudanum she had been entrusted to take unsupervised. Her husband, who had never paid her much attention to begin with, didn't even attempt to hide his relief, exclaiming, *Good God no!* when asked by the mortician whether he desired an open-casket service, but it was an answer that seemed to please the mortician and priest alike, for the smell soon became so bad that the corpse-surgeon was not able to enter his place of work without retching and the body was disposed of quietly some days before the ceremony and a casket filled with soil was blessed and interned in the family plot instead.

Sugar was only a third of the way through the bottle when I emerged soot-streaked from the crowd and joined him at the table. My eyes stung, lids puffy, swollen, almost closed. I wiped my nose on a sleeve so tattered it hung to my knees. I kept looking around, twitching like I needed to move though I was trying my best to keep still. I picked up the bottle of whisky and poured it into an abandoned mug and downed it in one without grimacing. Even Sugar, whose palette had been destroyed by a lifetime of tobacco, rum, grog and salted biscuits, struggled to stay composed when drinking straight moonshine, especially one as downright foul as that.

—Holy shite that's boggin, I gasped. Next time I piss it's going to be through a hole in my side.

Though I said this without humour, the thought made Sugar smile. I sat back in the chair, the constant need to move having lessened. I reached for the bottle but Sugar picked it up first and poured a more sensible measure than my first. Already my eyes were glazing over.

—Take your time, he said.

I swallowed the microscopic, by comparison, measure and held out the mug for more. Sugar obliged, then topped up his own glass and sat the bottle on the table.

—What's wrong with your eyes?

Sugar took out his pouch of tobacco and stuffed a pinch of it into his cheek. Then he tossed the pouch to me. I looked at it on the table, waited for the shakes in my hands to subside before snatching it up and poked a ball of tobacco behind my lips. But then I took a drink before it had congealed and ended up swallowing half of it as it came apart in my mouth and I gagged and retched at the strands caught in my throat, my hands not shaking any less than before. I washed it all down with another gulp of whisky, and another, then sat swaying in my chair.

—Are you alright? You look like you've a belly full of angry bees.

—The fuck's a bee?

—You don't know what a bee is?

—If I knew what a bee is I would have said, You know what, you're right, I do look like I've swallowed a whole bunch of angry bees but that sure isn't what happened. But I didn't, did I? I said, What the fuck's a bee?

—It's an insect. Yellow and black stripes. Fucks flowers, makes honey.

—You see any flowers round here?

—Beneath the snow?

—Fuck off.

—Are you alright?

—I need more whisky.

I held the bottle upside down over my mug to catch the single drop that came out.

—Haw, barkeep, I hollered over the din, waving the empty bottle above my head.

The man next to me took this as a threat and pushed me so I fell back into the chair. Sugar stood, one hand raised in apology, the other on my shoulder to keep me seated. The man was not local. Too well-dressed. He turned back to his companions and squeezed the arse of a passing whore on the arm of some honorary Laird celebrating another successful eviction.

—I thought it was just sheep you fancied! somebody shouted.

The Laird turned and grinned, already pulling his knob out over the top of his breeks, halfway up the stairs.

—Ah need a drink, I spat.

—As do I, seeing as how you drank mine.

—Then get some.

—You'll only drink it.

—That's what it's there for. Drink's for drinking and money's for . . . moneying.

I was on my feet again, empty bottle above my head, making my way to the bar. The man who had pushed me before ducked but not quickly enough and the glass bottle bounced off his head.

—You! he shouted.

—You! I roared back. What the fuck do you want?

—You better watch yourself, lad.

I held my arms out, looked myself up and down.

—What are you doing?

—Watching myself.

—Cheeky shite, said somebody else.

—Square go, said the man, rolling up his sleeves.

—I don't even know what that means.

—Outside, now.

—Fuck no. You been out there? It's cold as anything. Snowing, last I saw.

The man drew back his fist to hit me. Sugar caught it, meaning to stop the fight before it got started but I took the opportunity to smash the bottle over the man's head. The man wobbled for a bit before dropping to the floor. Sugar rolled his eyes. I said thanks. Then the man's pals piled into us. I jabbed the broken bottle at anybody who came near. Sugar roared in some foreign tongue and swung tables and chairs and glasses and bottles and people and anything that came near him, making no attempt to get anywhere, the two of us stuck in a corner of the bar till we were forgotten about in the ruckus that had broken out. I sank to the floor only half-conscious of the mayhem.

The hull is broken.
He tugs at the chain and is disappointed, though not surprised, to find it still attached.
There is another rumble, and then a crack and a flash of light and the boat seems to float, the passengers suspended in mid air till their chains heave them back to the floor with a crash. Those who were awake and able to, begin to panic as the ship violently pitches and rolls and water pisses in from all directions. They struggle to stand, climbing over one another in their haste to escape but, finding themselves trapped, yank at the chains or attempt to manipulate their swollen feet through iron shackles, wishing—if only for the moment—that their own flesh was rotting like it was on some of the people around them so that it would just slough off without resistance and their foot could pass through.

When I woke, Sellar and ten or so guards from the Watch stood over me. Sugar was gone. My face was bruised, could feel it swollen beneath my fingertips. The dried blood made me itch. A blooded bottle of whisky rolled on the floor between us. Sellar trapped it beneath his foot. He tried to crush it, kicked it away when he couldn't. Then he kicked me hard where he thought I had testicles. I didn't flinch. Instead, I said, Morning, and stuck a pinch of tobacco into my cheek.

They took us to the chief's house. They sat me at one end of this enormous wooden table and the chief sat at the other. At my right was Sellar, grinning. At my left, Sugar.

Sellar gestured towards the spread on the table, the wine, the glasses.

—I'm afraid you will have to help yourself to a drink, he said. The chief's servant is not well at the present moment.

My chained hands were in my lap. I put them on the table. Sugar's hands were free.

I had only seen the chief a few times before in person. My father took me once to a clan meeting— whether the meetings stopped after that or my father stopped taking me, I didn't know. After what I saw either reason would have made sense. The chief's bonnet was crumpled on his head like it had been squished into place, sodden, struggling to keep its shape, his plaid weighed down by the rain it had absorbed on the way into Badwater from his house up on the hill. Standing ceremoniously before us, flanked by his two guards, he had barely said a few words before this fisherman from Badbae pushed his way to the front with his clenched fists held aloft, shouting, Where the fuck were you?

He wasn't the only one.

—You're s'posed tae protect us!

—Instead ye let they bastards in!

—Bastards!

—Fuckin prick ye!

—Useless cunt!

The clansmen, fishermen, former soldiers, each with their own grudge against the chief, hurled long-gestated insults at him and his guards, jostling each another, trying to be the one at the front whose spit it was the chief wiped from his face. His guards pushed back the crowds, then one of them jabbed a bit too hard with his ceremonial spear and stabbed one of the villagers in the gut, enough that when he withdrew the spear the rest of them could see that he had drawn blood and, before you knew it, the guards were disarmed and held down. The chief had cowered beneath his ceremonial shield but was pulled out by the ankles. He clawed at the dirt and dug out a stone, which he flung pitifully and yet when it bounced off Glengarry's forehead, Glengarry had erupted like he had been pierced by an arrow and started laying into the chief, fists digging in so deep it seemed like he was trying to pull out the man's insides, and, seeing this, the others joined in as well and it was not long until one of the guards was dead, skull shattered by the stamp of a boot against a rock. Some of the crofters tried to pull the fighters off the chief, some of them joined in, some of them started fighting each other, all elbows and swinging hands and butting heads, not caring who they hit or whether they had been hurt. Then, as abruptly as it started, they dispersed, holding one another up as they staggered home or for a drink, some of them on their knees, shaking heads, smiling . . . The body of the guard who had been killed was thrown upon a fire.

Sellar smiled queerly and took a sip from a carved goblet that resembled a human skull.

—You want to know if it's real.

He raised the cup like he was toasting something.

—It is.

He pursed his lips and sipped.

—Does it look different to you? Unusual, strange? In comparison to other skulls you might have seen.

I shook my head.

—I know, he said. I was disappointed too. I had expected there to be a great deal of difference between an enlightened skull and that of a savage. Other than the single eye socket, obviously.

He finished his drink and tipped the cup upside down, shaking the last few droplets onto the rug.

—Look, he said, poking a finger inside. See those markings, those scrapings? Those are from a spoon, or whatever archaic tool these primitives used instead of a spoon to scoop the brains out and eat them. Your question, I can see it in your eyes, is whether it was me who ate this man's brain?

He closed his eyes.

—Sadly not, he sighed. However, he looked up, I am in the process of making arrangements with an Irish family to visit, with their son, a region where some tribes still perform acts of cannibalism and human sacrifice, who eat the flesh of their enemies and their friends alike, family members even, believing that doing so will provide them with the best qualities of those they digest. I have it on good authority that a fellow with an open-mind and even a modest purse can purchase one for consumption. I have not yet decided whether I will partake in such a delicacy but I certainly intend to observe and record the practice. I read that human flesh tastes somewhat like veal, a meat that I am particularly fond of. This description was of the white meat, however, from a sailor who had eaten a cabin boy during an extended period in the doldrums.

—I once saw a man pay a boy to eat slices of his own face, I said, though it was Sugar who had told me this.

—Have you ever tasted human flesh? Sellar asked.

—Not in the way that you mean, said Sugar.

It was the first thing he had said. The first time he had even looked up.

—Ah, you're making a joke. You've tasted a woman, of course. And likely men too. Being a sailor.

He waited for a reaction. None came. Then he pushed himself up from the table with a flourish and took from his inner pocket a small vial. The lid was triangular, with an eye painted on each of its three faces.

—No, he said, this is the closest I have come to tasting human flesh. Thus far. It's a tonic made from the preserved bodies of a pharaoh. I've become rather fond of it. He poured a small amount into his brandy and drank it down. I saw him stifle a gag as he swallowed, though I could not tell if it was from the tonic or the brandy. I cannot tempt you?

He wiggled the vial in Sugar's direction, then mine.

—No? Suit yourself.

He screwed the lid back on with some difficulty.

—You know that's not pharaoh what you're drinking?

—Excuse me?

Sellar put the vial down. Then he gripped both edges of the table and glowered at Sugar.

—You think you're drinking the ground remains of an Egyptian king, said Sugar. You're not.

—You don't know what you're talking about.

—I have knowledge in these matters. You name it, I've taken payment for putting it in the hold of a ship and transporting it across the world. It was fashionable, for a time. It was rare and therefore expensive. Of course, the more they wanted it, the less of them there were, which made them rarer, more expensive, more desirable. Mummified kings are not potatoes. You can't just dig them out the ground.

Sellar swirled his drink.

—You think you could tell the difference between the ground-up remains of a three-thousand year old king and a slave girl thrown on a fire, even before it was dissolved in vinegar?

Sellar stopped swirling.

—You think you're inheriting the qualities of some great leader, a god on earth, but all you've inherited is the knowledge that it is always better to go willingly.

—That's enough.

—When your customers can't tell the difference, why go through all the hassle of getting them the real thing?

—Enough!

Sellar sat down. He wiped his mouth with a napkin.

—You know there's a significant reward for your capture. As soon as these sheep-shaggers have been shipped to the colonies I'll have finished my work here. With what I've been paid, along with my reward for your capture, I'll be able to settle comfortably in the Americas. The south, I hear, has a particularly hardy workforce.

He turned to the chief who appeared to be asleep.

—Have you ever considered it, your Lordship?

—What? the chief grunted.

—Moving to America.

—No.

—Ignore him, Sellar said, back to his sing-song voice. He's in a foul mood. We have had a disagreement.

What I'd like to know, Sellar hissed, is whether you had always planned to betray your people or whether it only occurred to you after they got home, when you already had what you needed from them?

—You're speaking out of turn, Sellar, the chief growled.

—How many did you lose?

—Not a single man died under my command.

—When you came home. How many left when they learned you'd lied to them? How many sold everything they had to get away? How many died on their way to wherever it was they were going?

—I didn't lie. Things changed.

—You did okay.

—When we came back it was different.

—The canal, the aqueduct, the sheep.

—The old ways had gone. Used to be we were left alone up here.

—How many families did you replace with sheep?

The chief spat a sticky stream of saliva. It clung to his beard.

—You're nothing but the chief of sheep.

Sellar's hollow laugh echoed against the flagstones.

—So we are in agreement, Sellar continued. I guarantee that you will do well from this venture. A sea-loch, a port, a gateway—*thee* gateway—to the colonies. Sugar, tobacco, people . . .

—I can't move them. Not again.

—You want to leave them on Badbae when they could be sunning themselves in the Caribbean?

—I'm not having them worked to death on some god-forsaken plantation.

—Good gosh, no. There are far more affordable alternatives nowadays. All we need are men to oversee the workers, make sure they work hard and don't escape, maybe dole out a little punishment now and then to keep them in line. Foremen, if you like.

—No.

—Ah, I understand. You worry that without them you won't be chief, will have nobody to rule. But you do own the land, don't you?

—In a way.

—Then you stand to do well from it. The canal, the sheep, the port . . . Your future is secure. The clan name will be preserved and your offspring—

—I have none.

—Then we shall find you a wife. A nice one . . . from down south. With teeth.

After dinner the chief slumped in an armchair by the fire. He would grunt in reply to a question if you shook him hard enough by the shoulder while you asked it but otherwise he might as well have been dead, but for the unhurried rise and fall of his chest. If you were to watch him long enough, however, you would see him lift a glass of whisky to his mouth and, if the glass ran dry, he'd refill it from the decanter tucked beneath his arm.

Sellar observed him for some time and then, as much out of curiosity as anything else, it seemed, picked up the decanter and brought it down on the top of the chief's head. That the bottle didn't break surprised us all. The chief's head split open at the back. The gulf between the two hemispheres widened and filled with blood. I nearly shat myself when he turned to look at me. He nodded as though in agreement with Sellar's chosen course of action and toppled backwards onto the stone floor with his skirts riding up around his oxters. When his bladder went slack from being dead, piss shot out his shrivelled cock and splashed upon his loose face, flattening his whiskers, ending with a dribble down his gilly shirt, his ruffled kilt, and, finally, his dried pubes, to which the piss clung like dew on a spider's web.

Sellar tittered and crouched beside the body. With one finger he transferred a drop of piss to his own lips, his tongue darting out to collect it before it ran down his knuckle. Then he stood and, with some difficulty, picked up the chief's sword. With a foot on either side of the corpse, he raised the sword, let it fall, let gravity pull the blade to the floor, to the chief's head, disappointed to find that it did not slice cleanly through the skull like he had imagined—like the Oriental swords he'd read could slice a man diagonally in two, from the collar to the hip, without even trying—only crushed the chief's nose, dented the face a little, though he was amused by the sudden appearance of bloody worm-like snotters from his nostrils and the corners of his eyes, like they'd been hiding, waiting for just the right moment to jump out and shout *keek-boo* in a high-pitched voice.

I picked up the nearest bottle on the table and drank till I needed to take a breath.

The ship drops.

He is lifted through the air again. He falls, tumbling over a body beside him. He collides with the hull, is slammed against the floor. There is a crack and a slow groan as the ship struggles to stay in one piece, the sounds of it splintering, battered again by the sea, lifting, falling—

I told you we were goin somewhere, shouts a man across the hull, and Sugar agrees, it does feel like they are going somewhere, sensing the ship's movements as it lists, lifts, drops, rises and falls, when, with a tremendous roar, a rock breeches the bottom of the hull, broken planks and fractured wood caving in, and the man who spoke is impaled through the arse by a broken beam, which emerges from between his parted lips and holds him in his place like a spit-roasted mermaid.

An impenetrable cloud cloaked the land, stretching out to the sea where the cries of the women and children could be heard amid the chaos of dogs barking, snapping at the legs of frightened livestock that tumbled from the rocks amid the chaos, the soldiers a misshapen mass, a dark splodge of blue upon the cliffs, neighbours dragging the old and the infirm from their homes before the fire could reach them. The Watch made their way through Badbae serving justice as they saw fit. Most of the men were missing or had fled since the raid and the ones who remained were injured, leaving the women and their bairns to defend themselves, pack their meagre belongings.

> *Prisoners are smashed against the hull and knocked unconscious. They land face-up or down in the water. One prisoner hits his head against an overhead beam with enough force that his neck snaps. The ship rolls. Sugar grips the chain around his ankles in both hands, unlike the flailing contortions of those chained alongside him. The water that had seeped through the planks beneath their feet now pours in from above.*

Families huddled in the snow to watch the fire consume their homes. More than a handful of crofters and soldiers alike fell from the narrow crag into the sea or the loch. The waves that crashed into the cliffs froze above their heads and fell into the smouldering ghetto as sheets of glass, shattering into a thousand pieces.

> *Sugar drags himself onto the muddy bank of the river. He gasps for air and retches up black water. The glow from the torches of the guards across the river illuminates the final shapes of the ship before it sinks. Passers-by stop to look, point. Some of them laugh. Sugar crawls away from the river, swimming through the mud like an amphibian. The shackles round his wrist and ankles disintegrate and fall away.*
> *He stands, starts walking.*

—Well if she doesn't want to leave, we shan't make her, said Sellar. Guard the door, but do carry on.

—Aye, sir, replied the soldier, putting his torch to the grass roof of a croft.

—You can't do that!

He'd made me follow him, to watch as he rounded up my kin and had them beaten and dragged out into the sea. My hands were tied behind my back. Up to then I had taken it all in with my jaws clenched shut, just a swaying of my head. I'd been expecting it.

—Why, silly child, said Sellar, Of course I can.

—She's still in there!

The old woman had refused to leave.

Sellar ordered two soldiers to stand guard. Then he cut me loose.

—Watch, he said. Then, to one of the soldiers, he added, See that she does.

Black smoke rose from the thatched roof, the ends of the straw singed black, glowing orange in the darkness. But the old woman inside stayed silent.

I saw Sugar among the shadows, saw him helping a woman into a boat. I tried to go to him but one of the soldiers grabbed me by the neck and made me watch the burning croft, saying, You're no goin anywhere, laddie, and when I tried anyway he clubbed me in the eye with the butt of his rifle and I fell to the ground, socket brimming, feeling the jagged edge of the bones scraping against my eyeball. Smoke spilled from the burning house. I could hear screaming but it did not come from in there. I clawed at the feet of one of the soldiers, felt myself being dragged away, felt my hair come out, plucked from my skull like a torn fishing net. The barrel of a rifle in my mouth. Hearing one of them say, You know what lads, I don't think this one's a lad after all. Laughing. They let go of my hair, took the gun out my mouth, let my face fall into the cool mud. I rolled onto my back.

Sugar had the rifle.

At his feet a soldier was missing half his face. It was there somewhere, I knew, but arranged in a way that would be impossible to put back the way it was.

Then Sugar's face changed. He touched the opening in his gut with his fingers and dropped to his knees.

Sellar stood grinning. I was between him and Sugar.

The smell of burning wood and meat filled the air.

The soldier guarding the door of the burning croft came forward but ignored me, his eyes on the man whose bowels had burst out his gut.

I lunged at the soldier, sunk my teeth into his neck and tore away the flesh. The man thrashed, his screams unheard above the noise of the women and children and barking dogs and the roar of the fires and the gunshots.

I took the pistol from his belt and held it outstretched in both hands, finger on trigger, barrel pointing at Sellar.

A neat hole appeared where his nose used to be, an aura of gore in the snow behind him, like a headdress, red tips on white feather.

I dropped the gun. I pressed the heel of my hand against the broken bones of my face, this unrelenting flow of black blood falling into the snow.

I curled up behind Sugar, unable even to cover his wound, from which protruded cuts of meat I had only ever seen at the markets. He hadn't moved since the bullet passed through him, through his gut, through his backbone, but he wouldn't take his eyes off me, even as hands grasped us both and lifted us over shoulders and carried us through the snow that fell with ash towards the boats waiting where the loch would soon meet the sea.

Two men: a detective and a prison guard.
The men step carefully between corpses, sprawling limbs, bellies swollen, skin burst and coming off in places, eyeballs pecked out by birds or nibbled at by crustaceans, barnacles stuck tight to exposed skulls—
There's some missing, he says to the young guard trying to keep pace beside him.
There might be some still in the wreck.
He points to a small boat by the bow of the sinking prison. There are two men on the boat. One of them pumps air through a hose held by the other.
How many?
Seven or eight.
Which is it? Seven or eight?
The guard hesitates. Seven, he decides, figuring they could always dispose of an extra body should one turn up. They had found a few upriver—one tangled in a fishing net, another blocking a sewer, and one that frightened the life out of a poor young woman when its arm appeared suddenly in the gap between two streets.
One of the men on the boat shouts and the other goes to him and together they pull at a fishing line till the corpse that had been hung on it by the unseen diver is safely onboard.
Six to go, says the detective.
The young guard smiles nervously.

THEN THE EXPLOSIONS BEGAN AND THE GROUND quaked beneath their feet as the bridge that kept the sea and loch apart began to disintegrate. Rock crumbled and fell in chunks into the loch and the waves that crashed from the other side caused the sea to piss through in great freezing spurts. Church bells clanged and they could not see for the sunspots in their eyes, but they came to see the water, slowly at first, run from the crack in the rock, the hole in the dam widening as more poured through before the entire lochan pushed the rock out of the way, flooding the ditch and pushing towards the bridge, taking the fractured remnants of the dam with it. The water tumbled from the edge of the bridge into the loch below, the shock wave building until it dashed the banks of Badwater, chewing the dirt and the earth as it hit. The river continued to flow over the unfinished bridge, the dry bed becoming quickly saturated and unable to withstand the weight and pressure of the water above it, crumbling and giving way. As the first arch fell it collided with the next, the water cascading over the sides of the bridge and into the street, washing away the trampled dirt and wooden planks, until only a single leg stuck out of the loch and half an arch extended from the hillside, protruding over the chief's house, threatening, a picturesque fall burrowing through Badwater, churning the earth until the pool it formed joined the loch, its bank rising steadily to meet the water cascading down the hillside from the reservoir, crashing through the inns and the hotels and the two competing brothels where men handcuffed to beds drowned or were carried away on top of them down stairs or out of windows, bodies thrown through banisters, arms clutching at table legs, doorframes . . . In the loch, stone pillars teetered on floating boxes bobbing in the waves. Then a further explosion from the reservoir, one final detonation, an eruption creating an immense wave visible even on the departing ships, tearing through the snow like an avalanche, guided by the canal hacked into the valley and carried over the bridge into the loch, a tidal wave careering into Badbae crumbling into the water, water surging over the unfinished aqueduct, ripping up boards from the wooden roads and forcing loose the flat stones of buildings and toppling them, carrying away the sheep that displaced the people, leaving only the towers of the factories being built on the coast standing precariously without their scaffolding, which had been washed away.

Badwater, ablaze, disappears into the dark.

Sugar dug his fingers into his belly, the dark liquid leaking from him. His fingers black, moist . . . Hands gripping his wrists, ankles, dragging him away—

They're here,
someone calls out, panicking.
Get them off this ship,
says another.

> *Sugar took one by the hair, nails digging into his wrists.*
> *Fuckin savage bit me ye cunt!*
> *Smashed his teeth in with his boots.*
> *Eyes pleading.*
> *Aye. Get fuckin over there.*
> *Throw them overboard.*
> *Arse over tit—*
> *Waste of fuckin money that.*
> *No mine.*

The minister kneeling before him, face black with soot, eyes burning.

They're here, a sailor says.

—Aye, man. I know.

The Navy.
Lose them or lose the cargo.

The minister wouldn't say that.

Over it goes.

He finds one hiding below deck, fear in its eyes.
It goes for him.

Fucker's armed.
A broken-off broom handle.
Step sideways and take it from him, ram it into the cunt's
face, an eye, maybe, couldn't say

Still breathing.

Over it goes with the rest.

They're no stayin under, someone shouts.
Weigh them down, says another, hog-tying one with a chain,
kicking it over the side.
Here—

Someone rolls out a barrel and lassoes three monstrous
bastards to it. Over it goes, just rolled it, each of them getting a
face full of deck before the wallop of the cold sea.

He finds another, a young one, pretty too—not made for
working—cowering beside his bunk. Eyes pleading, bottom lip
quivering, glistening. She tries to smile, bats her eyelids . . .
He moves towards her slowly.
She turns her head, opens her mouth a little, pouting, eyelids
half-closed, and he reaches for her, places a hand behind her head,
gently, leans in like he's going to kiss her, runs her hair between
his fingers, clutches it, pulls it, tears at it while she claws at the
backs of his hands and pulls away, runs up the stairs, naked
across the deck,
bare feet slipping in the blood and saltwater,

over the side and

gone.

The others they slit their throats and shove them over, the water around them crimson, black bodies like bloated seal carcasses here and there as the other ship pulls up alongside.

The Captain shakes his head at the sight below, unimpressed but not disgusted, tellingly.

He spits.

Their hands behind their backs, in chains.
Back to shore, to the stocks . . .

The minister, standing up, book in hand. Blurred faces by his side, some looking his way, some not. He touched his gut—tight and dry, unable to tell where the dressing ended and his wound began, curdling its way inside him. The minister, kneeling again, stony-faced but his eyes welling, placed a warm hand on his forehead . . .

The boat threads through the blood.

Sugar wrenched himself upwards, tries to, spasms . . .

from the deck on which he lay
>*stinking and rotting of smoke and shit and things that humans aren't supposed to smell of—*

Smell on themselves.

He tried to spit up something but it stuck there at the back of his throat. The minister, sounding further way than ever. He strained to hear.
 —Speak up man, he asked, drowned out by the roar of the ocean, the boat rocking, creaking, sobbing.

He shivers.
 —Cold, he says, through chattering teeth and they pull a sheet over him, pitifully, grateful.
 More words from the minister. Then he closes his book and places his hat back upon his head.

The sheet, white over his eyes, inflating slightly with his raspy breaths . . . hands on his arms, strong but gentle. They lift him, talking, chanting—no, singing— onto their shoulders. He feels the wind, tastes the salt in the air, feels it against his skin as the blanket flaps and unfurls around him, and he falls, forever, the icy air whipping past, stabbing, the blackness swallowing him whole . . . he kicks out and thrashes his arms,

sees the blanket turn, ghostlike, swim upwards and away . . .

The light—

He reaches out, grasps it with his fingers, it closes around him—

> *. . . chains around his wrists and ankles, he kicks, kicks . . .*

—he spits, gulps and exhales on his way down, kicks off the rocks at the bottom—

> *. . . went under like the fucking cannonball he was tied to.*

> *The floaters they shot.*
> *Let em fill with water. That was the thinking.*
> *Almost worked too till they started bobbing up again from the gas in their bellies . . .*

He gulps for air, shudders as the cold envelopes him, pulls him under . . . Feels his boots in the sand.

Looking up, sees the hull of the ship pull away—

> *. . . sees their faces refracted by the water . . .*

—sees them peering over the side. Sees

her.

Me.

> *Sees them,*
> *hunched,*
> *distorted,*
> *hands*
> *curled like claws,*

as they set upon him . . .

When she'd finished her story she accepted the hunk of bread that was offered but when she went to take it her arm broke off at the elbow and crumbled like charcoal, bicep twitching. Her mouth moved like it was chewing, straw beard undulating when she swallowed, but the bread had fallen to the ground. In the morning only a clump of mulch remained, perched on the stone on which the she had sat. Hidden in the grass was the black pebble of her ghost eye.

Acknowledgments

Thank you to my granny, to whom this book is dedicated; to Alex, for your support and help with editing this book and for taking the precious time to read the previous one and letting me know what you thought; to Simone from Hedera Felix (publisher of Mycelia, which I highly recommended) for the very generous things you had to say about *But God Made Hell*; to Euan, my editor, for your enthusiasm and encouragement; to Austin James, author of *The Drip Drop Prophet*; to James McCulloch, writer of *City of Lost Souls* (and many other things) for the blurb; to my parents, my sister and her three boys for always being there (and helping out with childminding so I could get some of this done); to my amazing wife, Hannah, and our son, Louis, for everything, every day; and, finally, Steve Erickson, who doesn't know me, for showing me what is possible.

Stephen Toman lives in Scotland with his wife, son, and two cats. Previously, he has worked as a dish washer. *The Philistines Be Upon Thee* is (chronologically) the first book in the *Badwater* trilogy. *But God Made Hell* is the middle book.

MALKI PRESS
EDINBURGH

Malkipress.weebly.com
malkipressedinburgh@gmail.com
@malkipress

Also available from Malki Press:

Smoke Over Snow Angus Gunn

A Girl in a Pool Euan McBride

A Knife Fight in the Front Garden Louise Meldrum

But God Made Hell Stephen Toman

Printed in Great Britain
by Amazon